I WANNA BE YOUR SHOEBOX

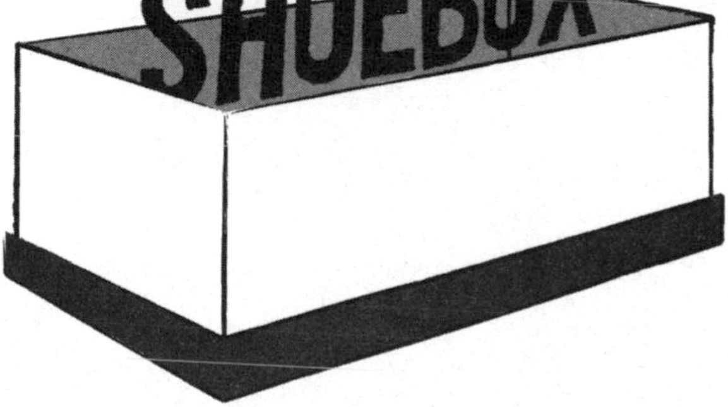

I WANNA
BE YOUR
SHOEBOX

CRISTINA GARCÍA

SIMON & SCHUSTER BOOKS FOR YOUNG READERS

New York London Toronto Sydney

SIMON & SCHUSTER BOOKS FOR YOUNG READERS
An imprint of Simon & Schuster Children's Publishing Division
1230 Avenue of the Americas, New York, New York 10020
This book is a work of fiction. Any references to historical events, real people, or real
locales are used fictitiously. Other names, characters, places, and incidents are products of
the author's imagination, and any resemblance to actual events or locales or persons, living
or dead, is entirely coincidental.

Book design by Lucy Ruth Cummins
The text for this book is set in Edlund.
Manufactured in the United States of America
2 4 6 8 10 9 7 5 3 1
Library of Congress Cataloging-in-Publication Data
García, Cristina, 1958-
I wanna be your shoebox / Cristina García. — 1st ed.
p. cm.
Summary: Thirteen-year-old, clarinet-playing, Southern California surfer Yumi Ruíz-Hirsch
comes from a complex family—her father is Jewish-Japanese, her mother is Cuban, and her
parents are divorced—and when her grandfather Saul is diagnosed with terminal cancer, Yumi
asks him to tell her his life story, which helps her to understand her own history and identity.
ISBN-13: 978-1-4169-3928-3 (hardcover)
ISBN-10: 1-4169-3928-8 (hardcover)
[1. Identity—Fiction. 2. Racially mixed people—Fiction. 3. Grandfathers—Fiction.
4. Family—Fiction. 5. California, Southern—Fiction.] I. Title.
II. Title: I want to be your shoebox.
PZ7.G155624Ias 2008
[Fic]—dc22
2007019344

"I Want to Be Your Shoebox" (pages 30, 152, 174, 175, and 185) from *Notarikon* by Catherine
Bowman. Copyright © 2008 by Catherine Bowman. Excerpted and reprinted with permission of
the author and Four Way Books, www.fourwaybooks.com.

Excerpt on pages 37–38 from *Part Asian 100% Hapa* © 2006 by Kip Fulbeck. Used with
permission of Chronicle Books LLC, San Francisco. Visit ChronicleBooks.com.

"Keats in California" (page 188) from *Breath: Poems* by Philip Levine, copyright © 2004
by Philip Levine. Used by permission of Alfred A. Knopf, a division of Random House, Inc.

FOR PILAR (AGAIN)
AND
HER GRANDFATHER AL BROWN
(1913–2006)

Every time an elder passes, a library is lost.

—African saying

"Will you walk a little faster?" said a whiting to a snail,

"There's a porpoise close behind us and he's treading on my tail.

See how eagerly the lobsters and the turtles all advance!

They are waiting on the shingle—will you come and join the dance?

Will you, won't you, will you, won't you, will you join the dance?

Will you, won't you, will you, won't you, won't you join the dance?"

—Lewis Carroll, *Alice's Adventures in Wonderland*

Don't you wish sometimes that everything could stay the same forever? A perfect moment stretched out for the rest of your life? Why do things always have to change so much, anyway?

My name is Yumi Ruíz-Hirsch, and my grandfather is dying. It feels funny to call him "my grandfather" because from the time I could talk, he insisted that I call him Saul. Nobody else I know calls their grandparents by their real names. Saul is Jewish, and my grandmother is Japanese and she's twenty-five years younger than him. Her name is Hiroko, and I call her by her first name too. When I tried calling my mother "Silvia," she refused to answer me. She's Cuban (with a little Guatemalan thrown in), and nobody in her family calls their elders by their first names. Mom says this mix of identities makes me a poster child for the twenty-first century.

Saul turned ninety-two on August 21. This was the day the doctors told him he had lymphoma. They said that the cancer was spreading all over his body and that he had maybe five or six months to live. Saul's reaction was very matter-of-fact. *Get me outta here.* That's how Saul talks, always fussing and complaining, but he's a softie inside. Saul says he doesn't want chemotherapy or anything else that might make him live longer. Basically, he doesn't want to suffer. He doesn't believe in pointless sacrificing either, so when the doctor told him to cut out his daily steak and cigar, Saul stormed out of his office without saying good-bye.

Mom told me about the cancer on my last day of surf camp. After a month of begging, I finally convinced her surfing wasn't too dangerous. She wanted me to take up ballet again, which I'd dropped the year before. If I never see another leotard again, it'd be fine with me. It wasn't the ballet that was so bad, but the girls who took it. They cattily competed over everything, like who starved themselves the most or got the best parts in the annual production of *The Nutcracker*. For my last role I was the lead mouse in the Christmas scene. I had to wear this bulky costume and a rubber rodent mask that gave me a heat rash. *Any performance is as good as its smallest part,* Mom encouraged me, but I didn't believe her. Saul was the only one who was honest about it. *Why'd you let them make you a rat?* Hiroko tried to shush him, but Saul isn't one to be so easily quieted.

Surfing is another world altogether. You're out on the ocean, feeling the power of the waves beneath your board, and it's just you and your thoughts and the big blue sky. I feel so free out there, like a seagull or a dolphin, and I forget all the things that are changing. Like the fact that my mother has a serious boyfriend and that my father is getting more depressed (he and Mom got divorced when I was a year old). Or that it looks like we might have to move (Mom and I live in this great house right on the ocean, but our crazy German landlord keeps raising the rent). Or that I'm about to start eighth grade, and if we move, I'll end up in high school with no friends. Or, most important of all, that Saul is dying.

When Mom came to pick me up that last day of surf camp, I was still floating in the sea. I saw her anxiously patrolling the beach and knew something was up. Suddenly, Mom starts waving her arms frantically and screams at the top of her lungs: "Sharks! Sharks!" I wanted to die of embarrassment. Then she screams it in Spanish for the convenience of the bilingual passersby: *"Tiburones! Tiburones!"*

My mom is a writer and has a highly overactive imagination. What she *did* see was a pair of dolphins cruising past the second break of waves, but she insisted that their dorsal fins looked identical to sharks' (they don't). *You'll understand when you have your own child* (I won't). I finally had to paddle to shore to calm her down.

To make matters worse, the surf instructor asked her to take a farewell photograph of our group. "Cowabunga!" she chirped, snapping the picture. Everybody smirked or rolled their eyes.

Afterward we went out for ice cream. That's when she told me about Saul. My eyes got all teary. How could this be happening? But it was. I asked Mom how my dad was taking it. *Well, you can imagine.*

Dad and Saul aren't exactly close. Dad lives in a run-down loft in Venice with our English bulldog, Millie. He's been composing songs for years but hasn't sold any, so he tunes pianos to pay the rent. Dad plays electric bass with a punk band called Armageddon, and he's the oldest guy by far. Mom says he should write a memoir about being a middle-aged punker, but Dad doesn't find this funny. He doesn't find anything she says very funny lately. Her fourth novel is getting published next year.

When I go over to my dad's on Saturday, it's dead quiet. There's no music blaring. His six electric basses and guitars are resting neatly on their stands, untouched. Even the Jimi Hendrix poster looks subdued. He calls me Yumi, instead of his nickname for me, Yummy. I wince whenever he says it in public, but today I miss it. I was named for Hiroko's younger sister, who died during World War II.

"How's Saul doing?" I ask my dad.

He hesitates for a moment, like he's not sure how much he should tell me. "Hanging in there."

I try to imagine what death might be like. I'm guessing it's kind of like a long sleep you never wake up from, but I know there must be more to it than that. My parents aren't raising me with any religion, so I'm not sure what to believe. My mom was baptized a Catholic and went to Catholic schools, but she doesn't believe in the usual things. Basically, she thinks that living things are imbued with a spiritual energy that is recycled into the universe after they die. So this could mean I'll eventually end up as part of a daffodil, or a cow, or a cloud.

I wonder what Saul might become a part of when he dies? More than anything, he loves going to the racetrack, so maybe, if he's lucky, he'll become a champion racehorse, a Triple Crown winner. Yeah, that would be perfect for him.

After our regular meal of instant vegetarian ramen noodles and peanut butter crackers, Dad and I go skateboarding for an hour or so, taking in the scene down the Venice boardwalk. All the regulars are there: the musclemen and the granny with six Chihuahuas dressed as circus performers. A new fortune-teller with a shimmery red headdress calls out to me: "Come, my precious, there is love in your future! My crystal ball never lies!" Then she turns to my dad: "And I see success written on your face!" He grumbles back: "Yeah, it's probably Tabasco sauce."

I'm half watching where I'm going, half watching the ocean, which is perfect with waves. There's a nice breeze, steady as a metronome, and it's bringing them in at about two feet high.

I try to picture what it must've been like on this very beach thirty years ago. It was the Dogtown era then, and all the kids surfed Bay Street and were revolutionizing skateboarding. Did they know it was a revolution?

I wish I could drop everything I'm doing and go get my surfboard (it's a dinged-up old longboard Dad found for me at a yard sale), but I'd feel bad about leaving him alone on the beach. Dad doesn't swim, and it kind of makes him nervous to watch me surf because he couldn't save me if something went wrong. When I tell him about my mom screaming about the nonexistent sharks, he laughs and shakes his head. "That sounds like your mother, all right." Then he adds, deadpan: "Look, I don't want you drowning in front of me, okay? I got enough on my mind as it is." You would have to know my dad to know that he's totally joking.

Later Dad is silent all the way up to Saul and Hiroko's house—no Clash or Ramones in the CD player. No playing his drumsticks against the steering wheel. He doesn't even play the taped show of our favorite radio program, *Jonesy's Jukebox*. The deejay, Steve Jones, is the former guitarist for the Sex Pistols. He has this gentle way about him and a funny cockney accent, and it's hard to remember that he's the same guy who called for anarchy in the U.K. Now Jonesy talks about his group therapy and his eating disorders.

Every Saturday afternoon we make this trip to Saul and Hiroko's house. They live out in the desert, about an hour

CRISTINA GARCÍA

north of here. Hiroko always prepares my favorite dishes: plain pasta with butter, avocado sushi, and sweet potato tempura. I help her in the garden too, raking the beds of pebbles in the front yard or wrapping mesh around the fruit on her trees. Hiroko is a huge believer in neatness. It's hard for her because I'm probably the biggest slob on the planet. Mom has pretty much given up on me, but Hiroko is hopeful I'll change.

Every Saturday, I bring my clarinet and Saul asks me to play whatever I learned that week. Then he really listens to me. His eyes never glaze over if I mess up a section or my reed squeaks. He doesn't tell me to practice either. He just listens and smiles, and when I'm done he says: *Yeah, kid, you're gonna be the next Benny Goodman. Mark my words.* It doesn't matter that I'm playing classical music or nothing he's ever heard before.

Saul told me he saw Benny Goodman play in Tokyo years ago. He tells me lots of things, mostly in bits and pieces.

Tonight, Hiroko goes all out with dinner, like it's a worldwide holiday or something. She's made brisket of beef, potato pancakes, tortellini with pesto, cheese enchiladas, couscous, and wonton soup.

What's all this?! Saul is confused by the dishes but settles down once he spots the beef. It bothers me that he eats meat, but nothing I tell him will change his mind. I became a vegetarian in third grade after I saw a film at school about the mistreatment of animals in the food industry. Lambs in cramped wooden stalls. Pigs carved up still twitching with life. Nothing could make me eat meat after that.

I put a sampling of most everything on my plate and dig in.

"So how's the piano tuning business?" Saul booms, like he's got a microphone implanted in his throat. He asks my dad this every visit.

"Same as always." Dad's words come out tightly squeezed.

"You gettin' any of your songs on the radio?"

Dad stops chewing and puts down his fork. "Not yet."

"My dad's got some great new songs," I chime in, trying to break the tension.

"You don't say?" Saul looks disappointed and drops the subject.

Dad and Hiroko don't say much during the rest of dinner. They're very alike that way. You have to read their faces to know what they're thinking. When Hiroko raises her eyebrows slightly, I know I've disappointed her (e.g., I've left dirty socks on the bathroom floor again). My dad might give me a hint of a smile to let me know he's proud of the riff I just played (he's teaching me to play electric bass, too). Only Saul speaks his mind. Each time I walk through the door, he says the same exact thing: *Hey, Yumi girl! It's good to see you, kid!*

Saul's a fireplug of a guy, barely five feet tall (I passed him by an inch last Christmas), with pale lips and papery skin and eyes so blue, they look like ice. The wisps of hair on his head are pure white and stick up in every direction. Nobody I know looks anything like him.

Sometimes I look at Saul and Hiroko and wonder what they have in common. Mom tells me the glue that binds two people together is a mystery. Saul is usually buried behind his newspaper, which he reads cover to cover, or analyzing the daily racing sheet, or taking a nap. Hiroko is busy in the garden or the kitchen, or she's cleaning, cleaning, cleaning. It's gotten worse since she retired from that electronics company last year. She proudly says that in her forty-three years of working there, she took only two sick days—when Saul had pneumonia. *She cared for me like a baby.* Saul beams every time she tells this story, and my grandmother smiles back at him.

After dinner, instead of settling in front of the TV for the Saturday-night lineup, I sit down next to Saul in the living room.

"So, kid, to what do I owe this honor?" he says with mock formality. He reaches into his pocket and pulls out a dollar to give me. "That should buy you a ride on a rickshaw." Then he laughs at his same old joke.

I nestle in beside him and—I can't help it—the tears begin to fall.

"Whoa, whoa there, little one! It's raining! Bring an umbrella! Bring a raincoat! We'll get as wet as a couple of noodles!"

But I can't stop. The tears burn down my cheeks, and my stomach starts churning like the time I got food poisoning in Cuba, and I feel like I'm going to throw up. Instead, I cry even harder. Dad and Hiroko come in from the kitchen to see what all the commotion is about. I can barely see them through the blur of tears, but I feel Saul's arm around my shoulder and his voice is soft.

"It's gonna be okay, Yumi girl. Don't worry. They can't get rid of me so easily. Ain't I from Brooklyn? Ain't I?"

I nod, my head still tucked under his arm. For Saul, being born and raised in Brooklyn is not just a happy accident of birth, it's proof of his toughness.

When I calm down, I look my grandfather straight in the eye and say: "Tell me everything."

"What do you mean, kid?"

"Everything, Saul. I want you to tell me your story, everything from the beginning. I want to hear about when you were my age. And about the time you drove that famous actress around Alaska. I want to know your whole life."

Then it was his turn to get teary-eyed. "Ah, what do you wanna know all that for?"

"Because I know who you are. But I want to know who you *were*," I answer.

And I can tell he's secretly pleased.

∞∞

When I was born in 1913, there was no such thing as a world war. Imagine that, kid. World War I hadn't started yet, and when it did, everyone called it the Great War, thinking it couldn't get any bigger. They were dead wrong about that. Now I ain't saying the world was innocent then, but it was simpler, a lot simpler. I grew up near Prospect Park, which was a fancy neighborhood for Brooklyn in those days. We were living good. My old man had a factory that made women's underthings—brassieres and corsets and whatnot—that sold down on Delancey Street for a couple of bucks. What's that? You don't know how to wear a corset? Do me a favor and ask your mother about that one, okay?

Like I was saying, we were living pretty good. Three-story brownstone a block from the park. An Irish maid who came in every day and complained about the mess I made. And we were one of the first families to have a car. I remember riding around in it faster than it seemed possible to go. I'm telling you, it felt like what a rocket ship would feel like for you today. My mother made me and my brother wear our winter hats the first time we rode in the car. Winter hats in the middle of July! Why, she was scared the wind would blow our ears right off our heads. We rode around Brooklyn like celebrities that day, honking and waving at everyone.

Well, everything good comes to an end. That's what they say, ain't it? My mother got real sick with tumors. It ain't like today, with all the chemo this and the radiation that. In those days it was a death sentence. Look, I'm ninety-two years old. I've lived my life. But my mother was thirty-eight, a beautiful woman. Big brown eyes with pink skin and her hands like two doves. Ruth was her name. Ruth Yenkel before she married my father and became Hirsch. I remember running home from school every day and climbing the stairs to her room. Every day I ran as fast as I could to make sure she was fine. My biggest fear was that she would die when I was at school and I wouldn't get to say good-bye.

My mother wasted away for two years. She started out a young woman and got old in two years, you know what I'm saying? Thirty-eight to sixty in two years flat. Her hair turned white, and her hands wrinkled up, and her eyes sunk down so deep, they looked like two faraway marbles. But it was her smell that changed the most. Smell your skin, Yumi girl, go ahead and smell it. Ain't it fresh-smelling? Best smell in the world, I'm telling you. In the end, my mother smelled old. No amount of perfume or talcum powder could hide it. My brother, Frank—he was four years older than me—couldn't tell, though. Scarlet fever killed off his sense of smell when he was a baby.

What I want to tell you is that on the day she died, I knew it ahead of time. It was a Tuesday in April. A gorgeous spring day that made you feel like nothing bad could happen. I was in eighth grade, just like you're gonna be, and I could hear Ma calling me. She was four blocks away, but I could hear her calling: "Saul, Saul, come home. It's time." I never ran so fast in my life. Not even later when I was chased by that moose in Alaska. Well, I flew home and up those stairs three at a time, and Ma was waiting for me. "Is he here yet?" she'd kept asking my father.

When she saw me, she squeezed my hand, gave me one last smile, and died right there with my head on her chest. Oh, I cried like a baby I did, even though I was expecting it. I'm not ashamed to admit it. Thirteen years old and I cried like a baby. It still brings a

CRISTINA GARCÍA

tear to my eye. Thanks for the tissue, Yumi girl. You're a good kid.

So as I was saying, the whole neighborhood came out for the funeral. Everyone was nice to us and brought over noodle kugel and rugelach and all the dishes that the good Jewish ladies made in those days. Our neighbor Elsie Blumenfeld and her three daughters brought more food than anyone. They knocked themselves out, too much so if you asked me, and it made me suspicious. Elsie had been widowed a couple of years earlier, and she told me she knew how I felt. She smiled when she said it, and I didn't trust her. Never trust nobody who smiles at you when they're telling you bad news. Take my word for it, kid.

Everything changed after my mother died. My dad married Elsie two months later, and she and her three daughters moved in with us. Frank went off to college that fall and ended up becoming a chemistry professor at Cornell. Go figure. A chemistry professor with no sense of smell. It's a miracle he didn't blow himself up. Elsie didn't waste much time changing things around to suit her. She moved out my mother's clothes and left them on the street for the ragpickers. Out went her opera records. Out went her bedding and the antique perfume bottles she collected. Elsie even pawned my mother's best jewelry and bought herself some gaudy butterfly pins from Brazil. The only thing Elsie kept of Ma's was her pearl necklace.

The two older daughters were nobodies, dull as a couple of Pilgrims. I couldn't tell them apart for the longest time. They had heavy, round faces with no expression whatsoever. You could've put them out to pasture and they would've started eating grass, you know what I'm saying? No offense to your cows, Yumi girl. Their idea of a joke was washing my long pants in boiling hot water until they shrank so much, I couldn't wear them no more. I can't remember their names. Give me a minute here, I'll try. Nah, they were too stupid to be evil stepsisters. This ain't no fairy tale I'm telling you. Okay, I remember now: Zelda was the oldest, then Sadie, then Juliet.

The little one, Juliet, was a sweet girl, the only decent one in the bunch. Nine years old, if I remember right. Sometimes when I was sent to my room without supper—Elsie did this to teach me manners—Juliet would feel sorry for me and sneak me a piece of brisket or a baked potato she'd wrapped in a napkin. Then she'd sit on my bed and watch me eat, careful to pick up any crumbs so I wouldn't get in trouble. She looked out for me. Nine years old and she was more maternal than her mother and sisters put together. I taught her how to play chess the summer they moved in, and Juliet got pretty good at it. Soon she was beating me more than half the time. Sharp cookie, that one. Much later I heard that she was the only one of the sisters to go to college. Majored in sociology or psychology or one of them ologies.

"I remember your mother," Juliet said once after she'd checkmated me again. "She was a real nice lady." Then she looked at me so tenderly that I cried as hard as when Ma died. She had a good heart, that Juliet. I couldn't say the same for them sisters, though. Mean and petty like their mother. Ah, listen to me moaning and groaning like Cinderella! The truth is, I had to grow up real fast around them, real fast, Yumi girl. I couldn't afford to be a mama's boy no more.

My father was no match for Elsie and them girls. So when Elsie decided that I was old enough to go out and work for a living, my father didn't fight her. Now I'm not talking about some part-time job scooping ice cream, but a real job, in a factory or on the docks, to help pay the mortgage. This meant I had to quit school. My father was losing a lot of money then. Hemlines were up and women weren't wearing corsets no more. Did you ever hear of the flappers? If my joints didn't hurt so much, I'd show you how to do the Charleston. Yeah, I cut the rug pretty good in my day. Like I was saying, them flappers—God bless 'em—were definitely bad for business. But this was nothing compared to what would come later, in the Depression. Everyone lost their shirts then.

It was no big tragedy for me to leave school. I never had no brain for book learning, and lots of kids were already working at my age. It's not like today, where you're nobody without a Ph.D. I keep telling your dad he should study more and get a good teaching job, cushy like my brother Frank had before he died. Three months off in the summer, holidays, benefits, everything. If you got the brains, it's the best job around. Anyway, I decided if I had to work, I sure wasn't going to bring home the bacon to Elsie and her daughters. So I left. Fourteen years old and out in the world. I know it's hard to picture that now, Yumi girl, but those were different times.

2 | SEPTEMBER

"SO SAUL STARTED TELLING ME THE STORY OF HIS LIFE," I SAY, grabbing another handful of popcorn. I'm at a sleepover at my best friend Véronique's house on a Friday night.

"Why?" She stares at me from under her Minnie Mouse ears, which she likes to wear to bed.

"I told him I wanted to know everything about him."

"Before he dies, you mean?"

"Well, I didn't exactly put it that way. But yeah, before he dies." When I first told Véronique about Saul, she cried uncontrollably. She reacts to everything a lot harder than I do, even if it's my tragedy. Véronique is also scared of a lot of things: spiders, and the exact stroke of midnight, and the doorbell ringing unexpectedly.

"My dad's grandmother lived to a hundred and six,"

Véronique says, trying to cheer me up. "And everyone told her she would die fifty times before that. She ate chocolate every day of her life too. At least a pound a day."

"Whoa! A whole pound? I wonder if Saul could eat that much chocolate?"

"That wouldn't be a problem for me," Véronique giggles. She eats all she wants and stays skinny as a pole. Her favorite food is butter. She'll eat it plain right off a dish. We met in first grade. Véronique sat next to me in the cafeteria and offered me half of her butter sandwich. *Ants don't like margarine, you know. Like us, they prefer butter.*

We became fast friends after that. We even joined orchestra together in sixth grade (Véronique plays the violin).

"He's told me all kinds of stuff about his mother dying," I continue, "and that he was kicked out of his house at fourteen. You never really think of old people having parents or ever being our age."

"My parents are ancient!" Véronique pops up like a jack-in-the-box. "I'm not supposed to tell anyone, but my dad's sixty and he dyes his hair."

"I'd noticed the dye job."

"Really?"

"Look, it's all relative. We're in eighth grade, and everyone's saying 'Yeah, we're top dogs this year' and lording it over the younger students. But the sixth graders look so small and geeky that I feel sorry for them. That was only two years ago for us. I don't remember ever being so clueless."

"But they *are* small and geeky," Véronique laughs.

We go to a big public middle school with two thousand kids from all over the city. There's lots of cute boys at our school, especially Eli, who only Véronique knows I like.

"So how's the foil ball going?" I decide to change the topic.

Véronique goes to her closet and emerges with a huge wad of foil and a measuring tape. She collects foil—she'll practically snatch it off your sandwich—and is shaping it into one really big shiny ball. "Nineteen inches in diameter," she says with satisfaction. "That's four inches bigger than a month ago."

Véronique's parents are getting a divorce and her older brother is autistic. When they go to family therapy, she says everyone yells at one another. I want to tell her that divorce isn't so bad. Then again, I don't have any memories of when my parents were still married.

"Do you wanna watch a movie?" Véronique asks.

"Sure." I don't feel like talking much anymore, but my brain doesn't stop. How would my life be different if my parents were still together? I'm always forgetting things at my mom's or dad's place and getting in trouble for being irresponsible. But how would they feel if they had to keep things straight in three places? Sometimes I wake up in the middle of the night and don't know where I am: in the twin bed at my dad's loft, or the pullout sofa in my grandparents' house, or the canopy bed at my mom's.

Until recently, my parents got along pretty well, but lately, things have gotten tense. First, Mom has this new boyfriend, Jim. Second, she wants to move up to the Napa Valley, where she bought a house years ago that she's been renting out. She complains that she's tired of living in Los Angeles and paying big-city prices for everything. That's fine for her, but I don't want to move. Why can't my mom just stay in one place until I go off to college?

In the morning Mom picks me up at Véronique's house with Jim. He's a music professor and orchestra conductor in Texas who went to one of her readings and fell in love with her. Mom likes to say that he's been her one and only groupie. So who does she think she is, a rock star? My mom has been single for almost twelve years, and it's not as if she's found anybody that great. She used to introduce her dates to me as "friends," but I knew what was going on. And as far as I know, my father hasn't gone out with anyone since the divorce.

It's been just me and Mom, or me and Dad, for so long that I don't want it any other way. I didn't ask to be shuttled back and forth between them, but I've gotten used to it. I don't really expect my parents to get back together, but don't make me deal with anybody else.

"Anybody want to go out for brunch?" Jim asks cheerfully. Apparently, he's here for the weekend again.

"No, thanks," I mumble.

CRISTINA GARCÍA

"Yumi, where are your manners?" Mom sounds annoyed.

"I said, 'No, *thanks.*' I'm just not hungry."

"That's fine, honey. Don't worry." Jim is only making it worse by being nice. "Do you want to go surfing? Maybe I can give it a try today."

I burst out laughing. Could Jim really think that I would set one foot on the beach with him and my mother?

"Maybe you can teach him how to surf, Yumi?" Mom's voice has an edge to it, but I'm not going to be railroaded into this.

I don't have many choices these days, so when I do have a choice, I'm going to fully exercise it. Let them torture me, deprive me of food, but I'm definitely *not* going surfing with Jim. Plus, there's no way I want to see him in a wet suit— ugh!

Then he suggests playing music together—he's a cellist, too—but I'm not interested in doing that, either. Why doesn't he just leave me alone?

"I've got a lot of homework." Hard to argue with that.

On Monday our music director drops a bomb on my life. Mr. Shuntaro holds up a green sheet of paper from the Los Angeles Unified School District and reads it to the orchestra in a stressed-out voice: "'We regret to inform you that our school district can no longer support both a concert band and an orchestra at Wilton Middle School. Effective immediately, your orchestra is officially discontinued.'"

There's a roar of protest and disbelief. No orchestra? Eli makes an obscene noise on his tuba. The bassoon player blows a mournful note, and the viola players all stand up and scream, "Noooo!" A couple of the violinists start weeping, and our first cellist, Alex Pavel, stalks out of the room. "We'll strike!" he threatens, raising his fist. "We'll walk out on them!" "That makes no sense," I call after him. "Striking means *not* playing. Isn't that what they're ordering us to do?"

Mr. Shuntaro tries to calm us down by jumping on a metal folding chair and screeching like a chimpanzee. He never does anything you expect him to do. Once in the middle of a bad rehearsal he started eating the sheet music, to make a point about "ingesting" our parts. He didn't pretend to eat it, but actually ate it, with a little salt and pepper he pulled from his duffel bag. But today even his chimpanzee act isn't cutting it.

"This is an outrage!" I shout and everyone starts chanting *"Out-rage! Out-rage! Out-rage!"* Quincy Kaler, one of the double bass players, takes out his cell phone and starts recording the whole scene. "I'm gonna send it to Fox News!" he yells over the din.

"Right on!" Véronique squeaks. (As outspoken as she is in private, I've never, ever heard her say a word in the two years we've been in orchestra.)

Mr. Shuntaro is trying to get our attention by waving a pink sheet at us this time. It's a petition, and he wants everyone's signature on it. I sign my name in huge, loopy letters and underline it twice. There's eighty-two signatures altogether. How can we lose?

When word spreads on campus that the orchestra is being dumped, the reaction is . . . a gigantic yawn of indifference. Turns out no one really cares about classical music.

Most of what I hear at school is really bad rap or really bad pop. I don't believe in extreme forms of punishment, but bad pop brings me close to the edge. I guess I'm at two ends of the musical spectrum. On the one side: first-rate punk and rock-'n'-roll (no poseurs, please); on the other side: Mozart, Mahler, and Tchaikovsky. Soon after I started playing clarinet in fourth grade, Mom took me to my first symphony.

You mean playing music can be a job? I thought.

I vowed right then and there it was what I would do. Yumi Ruíz-Hirsch, principal clarinetist of the Los Angeles Philharmonic. I like the sound of that. But how can I ever do that if the orchestra is gone?

We'll fight to keep it, do whatever we have to do.

After school Mom drives me downtown to shop for bras. She's a terrible driver and curses like crazy whenever she's behind the wheel. She says it's a form of Tourette's syndrome and tells me not to repeat anything she says. But it's hard to stay neutral when she swears at every car on the road. We're sitting in traffic when I break the news to her.

"There's no more orchestra, as of today," I say glumly.

"No more orchestra? Did they fire that Japanese guy?"

"The school district says it can't afford our orchestra anymore. All we have left is the concert band—and even that probably won't be around much longer."

"That's an outrage!" Mom swerves to avoid a collision with some crazed motorist speeding along the shoulder of the highway.

"That's the same exact word I used."

"So what are you going to do about it?"

"What can we do?"

"Plenty, *mi amor*. Plenty. You can't just let them do this to you from one day to the next. Let me call that PTA woman and see what can be done."

"I'm not sure it'll do any good."

"There's always a way. Didn't I get you those boots everyone wanted for half price?"

"This is different. Besides, do we have to go all the way downtown just for some underwear?"

"You know I don't—"

"I know, I know. You don't pay retail." This is one of her mottoes. My mom was born in Cuba but grew up in Brooklyn, like Saul. Her parents had a restaurant, and they bought everything wholesale: gallons of milk, sides of beef, dozens of loaves of bread. Even today, Mom has trouble cooking for just the two of us. She triples and quadruples recipes, then puts the leftovers in the freezer where they sit for years in a kind of Ice Age cemetery.

Mom asks me what else is going on at school. She doesn't even bother transitioning into the subject. She's as blunt as a hammer. I try to keep my answers to a minimum even though this frustrates her to no end.

It's nearly closing time when we finally get downtown. We race up and down the crowded streets filled with every imaginable article of wholesale clothing.

"Fancy shops on the Westside buy their merchandise here, then hike up the prices," Mom crows, fingering a pretty peasant skirt.

It's true. I've seen these same skirts going for seventy dollars on the Third Street Promenade. But most of what I see is junk.

Mom takes me into this one lingerie shop, and we head to the back, where there are racks and racks of pastel-colored bras suspended overhead like giant moths. She starts bargaining with the owner right off the bat. This is her idea of fun. She says the vendors don't respect you without a good fight.

"You need to buy at least six dozen to pay that price, Missus!" The owner has a thick accent and a mustache to match.

"Okay, I'll buy a dozen," Mom says.

"You no hear me?" The owner is getting agitated now. But Mom has taught me that this is all part of the game.

"Down the street they sell similar bras for less. But your quality is better, I can see that." She punches a cup for emphasis and smiles.

This softens him a bit.

"Ten dollars for the dozen, then?"

"Fifteen," he sputters.

"Twelve, but not a penny more."

"Okay, Missus, okay. If I have more customers like you, I go bankrupt. Kaput!"

Mom picks up the dozen bras (I only needed three) and looks at me, flushed with victory. "Hungry, sweetheart?"

A food cart outside is selling tamales and soft drinks. I ask for a plain cheese tamale, and Mom, of course, has to order the pork one with extra hot sauce. I glare at her but know better than to start one of my vegetarian tantrums in public. She's got zero problems making a scene. It's in her genes.

"What causes cancer?" I ask Mom later that night over hot chocolates. I'm wearing one of my stiff new bras under my pajamas, to break it in.

"Nobody knows for sure," she says softly. "Sometimes cells go haywire and start multiplying and attacking healthy ones for no reason. But there are cofactors like stress, poor nutrition, insufficient roughage, beta-carotene, antioxidants . . . "

The list goes on and on, and I tune her out. All I really want to know is why Saul is dying. I know you can't get to be ninety-two years old and have nothing wrong with you. But I wish a miracle would happen to make him better. Doesn't Mom always say that there are countless inexplicable occurrences in

CRISTINA GARCÍA

the world, things without rational explanations? When I was in Cuba with my mother, she took me to *santería* ceremonies. The priests and priestesses threw shells to tell the future and recommended potions for people who were sick. I was scared when I went to these ceremonies, but now I wish I could consult those same *santeros* about Saul. Maybe they could help him live longer, take away his cancer. Maybe they could make time stand still.

That's what I want more than anything in the world.

A little later most of my friends are online, so I check in. Talk turns to the orchestra, but nobody has any idea what to do. Should we protest? Write to our congressperson? (Nobody even knows who our congressperson is!) Cindy Grady offers to be our conductor, but she has enough trouble getting a decent sound out of her French horn. On a good day she sounds like a dying moose. We talk about circulating a bigger petition, but it's not like we can get much support at school. I suggest we try to raise a lot of money and keep the orchestra going ourselves. Go independent.

Suddenly, everyone is chiming in with ideas—a bake sale, washing cars, selling lemonade—but there aren't enough cupcakes in the world to keep a full orchestra playing for long. We'd be lucky just to subsidize our cork grease and reeds. *We have to think out of the box.* This is Quincy Kaler weighing in, and I agree with him.

How about a fund-raising concert? I suggest. *Maybe an all-girl punk band.* Dad says you can play punk with three chords and lots of attitude, so how hard could it be? I figure we could cover a couple of great Ramones songs, maybe write one of our own. Everyone gets excited about this, but nobody plays the right instruments. It's hard to imagine "Blitzkrieg Bop" or "Teenage Lobotomy" played on violin (Véronique or Lucy Kim), French horn (Cindy Grady), cello (Rachel Lehmer), bassoon (Zoë Hoffman), flute (Kara Winrow), and clarinet (me).

But in less than five minutes everyone is already fighting over a name for our nonexistent band. I'm in favor of Don't Call Me Miss. The other contenders are: Testosterone-Free Zone (TFZ), the Anastasias, Kisses for a Dollar, the Neo-Cramps, and Nasty Girls. Quincy complains that boys shouldn't be excluded from the band and says he'll play in drag if he has to. Believe me, at six foot two and one hundred seventy pounds, that would *not* be a pretty sight. We agree to keep brainstorming and finally sign off.

When Mom tucks me in for the night, she reads me a poem by García Lorca, her all-time favorite poet:

> The moon goes over the water.
> How can the sky be so tranquil?
> She sets about slowly reaping
> the river's ancient tremor

while a young frog takes her
for a tiny mirror.

I can't go to sleep for the longest time. We night owls get
the short end of the stick, even when it comes to surfing.
Everyone says the best surfing happens early in the morning,
but who knows what's going on after dark? I imagine owning
a long stretch of beach in California, or Hawaii, or maybe
even Australia, which I would light up at night with gigantic
spotlights. Then anybody who wants to could surf 24/7. We'd
have our own nighttime competitions and go to sleep when
the sun came up. Nobody would ever get sunburned. Yeah,
this is crazy enough that it might actually work. Maybe I'll
become world-famous and—

My fantasy is interrupted when I hear Mom on the telephone
with her sister, my tía Paloma, in New York. The two of them
troll Internet sites nearly every night looking at babies for
adoption around the world. Tía Paloma is only a year younger
than my mom, but she never had a baby and desperately wants
one. I hear them cooing about this baby or that, but so far my
aunt hasn't decided on just the right child. Then the phone
rings again, and I know it's Jim calling my mom to say good
night. It's hard to make out what Mom is saying because her
voice gets all soft and hushed. It makes me want to smash up
the phone. When I finally fall asleep, I dream that I'm night-
surfing a thirty-foot killer wave.

When I head over to my dad's place the next day, things are quasi back to normal. The music is blasting, and he's playing along to an old Social Distortion CD. The song, he says, is a cover of Johnny Cash's "Ring of Fire." I start dancing around, though I never really let loose in front of my dad. I try to get Millie to dance with me, but she scuttles off to her blanket and is snoring in no time. Dad tells me he's writing a new song for his band, inspired by an old Memphis Minnie recording. The liner notes explain that her famous line "I want to be your chauffeur" was transcribed years ago by some clueless musicologist as "I want to be your shoebox."

"What an idiot!" Dad laughs. "But I think I'm getting a good song out of it. The challenge is finding enough words to rhyme with 'shoebox.'"

He picks up one of his electric guitars, cranks up his Pignose amp, and starts singing:

I WANNA BE YOUR PARADOX
I WANNA BE YOUR PAIR OF SOCKS
I WANNA BE YOUR EQUINOX
I WANNA BE YOUR FORT KNOX

YEAH, YEAH, BABY, I WANNA BE YOUR SHOEBOX
LET ME BE YOUR SWEET SHOEBOX

"That's all I've got so far." He grins, waiting for my reaction. "Any suggestions?"

"Box of blocks?" I laugh, imagining some pimply guy sitting on the floor playing with blocks and crooning a love song.

"That's great, Yummy!" Dad's excited and taking notes.

"Bagels and lox?"

"Perfect! Perfect! I should've asked you sooner!" He rattles off some other possibilities for me to give a thumbs-up or thumbs-down on: *Your school of hard knocks?* (Up.) *Your case of smallpox?* (Maybe.) *The tick in your tock?* (Down.) *Your igneous rocks?* (Definitely down!) By now we're laughing so hard, it's impossible to talk. Then all of a sudden, Dad starts to cry. His face is wet and contorted, and I feel so scared and sorry for him that I don't know what to do.

"It's okay, Dad." I pat him gently on the back the way Mom does when she's putting me to bed. "It's gonna be okay."

*My first job was as a busboy at an Armenian restaurant on the Lower East Side. I didn't get no salary, just what the waiters felt like giving me from their tips. I was at their mercy, is what I'm saying. Some days I barely made two nickels. If it weren't for the fact that I got to eat one meal a day there, I would've starved to death. My favorite dish was the stuffed meatballs—*kufta, *they called them. But if I ate too many, the owner would start yelling at me in English and Armenian: "You make me broke! Enough* kufta *for you!" And worse things than that.*

Anyway, there was this old guy who used to come in every day for his lunchtime bowl of khash. It was basically a hoof, stomach, and tongue soup—the cheapest thing on the menu. This customer was always complaining: "The soup isn't hot enough! . . . There ain't no meat here—only hot water!" And so on and so forth. One day the waiters decided to get back at him and took turns spitting in his soup. They passed the bowl to me, and I spit in it too. If you can believe it, the guy loved his soup that day. He even asked if we had a new cook! We were laughing all afternoon about that one. The thing is, that customer never came back. I hope we didn't kill the poor guy!

Next thing I did was work in a button factory. I found out soon enough that I wasn't cut out for no nine-to-five. Ten minutes for lunch and some lout breathing down your neck every time you turned around. My hands cramping up with the piecework. The only good part was that I was surrounded by women, sweet-smelling gals who petted my cheeks. After that I started pushing racks around in the garment district. I think I lasted a month. It was hard work, but I liked being outside and all the hustle and bustle of the streets—and I was pretty fast. That job came to an end when I crashed a rack of clothes into a store window. Cost my boss ten bucks to replace the glass. That was a fortune in those days, believe me.

So what else did I do? Let's see. Ran errands for a big shot on Wall Street. Shined shoes for a day and a half in the hot sun. Worked for a Jewish newspaper in the basement mailroom, where I didn't see daylight for ten hours straight. Watered plants for a florist downtown. There were plenty of jobs in those days. But I didn't go more than a few weeks at a single one. Besides, I spent the money as fast as I earned it. I rented a tiny room in one of them tenements—nobody calls them that no more—and I got by on egg creams and coffee. What I liked to do most was wander around the Brooklyn docks and see the ships going in and out. But you had to know people to work on the docks. Besides, I was just a kid. It'd be a long time before I found my way to working in a port.

I spent a few years living hand to mouth in New York. I wasn't much older than you are now. What are your responsibilities? Cleaning your room? Doing your homework? Luxuries, little one. Yeah, you might be forced to move, but your mother's alive, ain't she? And she loves you, right? You don't know how good things are until you lose them. That's what I'm telling you—appreciate what you got, kid. I know there's lots of changes happening right now, but it might just work out for the best. You never know how closing one door can open another.

Like I was saying, Yumi girl, I learned to be a man on those New York streets, to keep an eye out for opportunity. Who knew when it was gonna knock? And I admit I had an eye for the ladies, too. I was starting to get interested in them, you see? Sixteen, seventeen. I was a good-looking boy, if I do say so myself. You're laughing? I know it's hard to believe now, kid, but I was handsome. All the girls loved Saul. As I've always said: Height means nothin' if you've got that certain somethin'.

I took a fancy to a pretty lady named Ethel Kleinman who sold shoes on Broadway. It wasn't no ordinary shop. They made shoes-to-measure for people with problem feet—you know, with corns and bunions or deformed in some way.

Well, I finally got the courage to ask Ethel to dinner. I wasn't expecting her to say yes right away, so I had to scramble to come up with enough dough to take her out. It's not like today, with everything split fifty-fifty. In those days, when a man asked a woman out, he paid from soup to nuts. Then, if he was lucky, he might get a peck on the cheek.

Now where was I? Okay, I needed to come up with some fast money, so my friend Marty Feldenberg says we should go to the racetrack. We take the train out to Long Island. Lots of classy people in the stands, not the riffraff you see today. It was a sunny day, and the grass was as green as I'd ever seen it, and the horses looked like gods thundering down the track. I thought, What can be better than this? It got even better. I turned five bucks into fifty in an hour. Another three hours of betting and I had two hundred more in my pocket. Never made easier money. Marty said it was beginner's luck, but I was convinced it was something else. A gift. I could look at a lineup of horses and know which one would cross the finish line first. I could tell who had the drive to be a winner. It wasn't always the favorite either. Well, I don't know where this gift came from, but let's just say my nine-to-five days were over.

Hear me out, Yumi girl: Whatever you want, you gotta go after it like them horses running toward the finish line.

3 OCTOBER

IT'S MY BIRTHDAY, AND I'M SURFING OFF BAY STREET ON my brand-new board, a six-foot four-inch Rusty. Well, I'm doing my best not to look too stupid. I'm still a beginner even if I like to think of myself as a surfer already. The gap between how I see myself and how I actually am is pretty huge. I've seen all these great surf movies—*Step into Liquid* is my favorite—and I love the idea of dropping down on a forty-foot wall of water. I've been covering my bedroom walls with posters of Layne Beachley and Kelly Slater riding the Pipeline, not to mention the top surfer in the world: Laird Hamilton. (Mom gets a heart attack just looking at them.) Of course, they're fighting for wall space with David Bowie and the Ramones.

Mom talked my *other* grandparents into getting me the

surfboard and a wet suit in advance of my birthday, an amazing feat considering they still think of me as a child. Everything arrived a week ago, wrapped so indestructibly that we could barely get the boxes opened. Abuela and Gramps, my Cuban grandparents, couldn't be more different from Saul and Hiroko. We're talking yin and yang here. They'll be coming out from Miami at the end of the month for my belated birthday/Halloween pool party.

I finally convinced Mom to let me throw a party, and I've been spreading the word. I've even invited a few boys from the orchestra: Scott Clare (trombone); Christian Wagner (cello); Mike Suzuki (tuba); and Billy "Las Vegas" (not his real name, on drums). Not to mention Eli and Quincy.

Part of the problem with me and surfing is that none of my friends do it. When I come out to surf, I go alone. Here we are living along one of the best coasts on the entire planet, and nobody I know wants to surf. The only person who's even mildly interested is Véronique, but she doesn't swim well enough. Besides, she has to babysit her brother after school.

Most of the surfers here—or anywhere, for that matter—are male. Not my age, but older, sometimes way older. I'm kind of curious about them. Most of these guys in Venice have been coming out to surf every day for years. (At least I see them every time I'm here.) They're not famous or anything, but they're really good and do it for the love of the sport.

I wonder if they knew Jay Adams and Tony Alva in their heyday. Why doesn't someone tell the life stories of the more ordinary surfers?

My dad's being a sport and watching me surf today because Mom is on one of her reading tours. October is Hispanic Heritage Month, so she gets lots of invitations from colleges to do lectures and readings. She likes to joke that she's a seasonal item, like the Easter Bunny or a Thanksgiving turkey. One of her best friends, a Nigerian writer, laughs that February is his big month, on account of Black History Month. It's twisted that people get divided up like this. So where's the month for people like me?

A couple of years ago my dad took me to get photographed for something called the Hapa Project. This artist wanted to do a series of portraits of people who were part Asian. That's what "hapa" means: "people of mixed racial heritage with partial roots in Asian and/or Pacific Islander ancestry." So this artist took pictures of me and my dad with our shoulders bare—and of dozens of other people, too—and turned it into a book. We also had to write on a blank sheet of paper our answer to this question: *What are you?* This is what I wrote:

> I am in 5ᵗʰ grade and I really like to read and write stories. I also love to write poems, here's one of them:

Is it Autumn
the brown leaves go tap tap
as they fall to the ground
Does it hurt the earth?
    I wonder,
        Is it autumn?

Here's what my dad wrote, all in capital letters:

WHAT ARE YOU? HARD TO SAY, EXCEPT MAYBE SELF-CONTAINED,
LEFTIST, AND HUMOROUS ... AND INCREASINGLY IMPATIENT WITH
THE NONSENSE OF OTHERS?

ACTUALLY, THE REASON THIS IS HARD IS BECAUSE I'M USED TO
DEFINING MYSELF, AND BEING DEFINED, BY WHAT I'M NOT. I AM A FATHER.
ALL OTHER CLAIMS TO INDIVIDUALITY SEEM FLUID OR DEPENDENT ON
THE CONTEXT. MAINLY, IT SEEMS THAT I AM WHAT OTHERS ARE NOT.

IS HAPA ENOUGH FOR YOU?

I'd never heard my dad use that term "hapa" before. Mostly, he says that he's half Japanese or that his mother is from Yokohama. I don't think I've ever heard him talk about the half of him that comes from Saul.

I'm disappointed that Mom's not here on my actual birthday, but I'm glad to be surfing. The surf is rough today, and I stay

CRISTINA GARCÍA

close to shore, trying to ride in on the whitewash. It's Friday afternoon, and I can hear people screaming from the rides on the Santa Monica Pier. The Ferris wheel is lit up, and the roller coaster is ratcheting along its track like an upside-down caterpillar. I love riding the roller coaster, but nothing is better than being out on the ocean with my surfboard. I wish I could stay out here forever.

Hiroko and Saul are waiting for us at my dad's place to take me out for my birthday. Millie sniffs everyone happily, then settles back down on her blanket after the big exertion. She doesn't have much of a tail, so when she wags it, the back half of her body wags along. She's the cutest thing. The only sad part about bulldogs is that they live only seven or eight years. We get them from the pound when they're grown already, so it doesn't give us much time together. Before Millie we had Big Boy, then Sally before him, and Frank, the original, was before her. I can't imagine having any other kind of dog. They're drooling, flatulent, lazy, and on the slow end of intelligence, but you won't find a more loving dog anywhere.

There's a big discussion about where to go eat, but we end up at our old standby: the Jewish deli/diner on Washington Boulevard. The same thing happens at dinner. Everyone talks about trying this and that, but everyone orders the usual.

Saul: a pastrami on rye with fries (over Hiroko's protests about his cholesterol).

Hiroko: a cup of vegetable barley soup with a house salad, dressing on the side.

Dad: an open-faced turkey sandwich with gravy, with or without the fries, depending on whether he's gone to the gym that week.

Me: grilled cheese and tomato with fries.

For dessert we order a slice of strawberry cheesecake to share and I get my regular dish of vanilla ice cream with rainbow sprinkles. I know it's boring, but there's something comforting about knowing what to expect. Tonight there's a candle in my ice cream and the waiter sings to me in a scratchy baritone, stopping once for a coughing fit.

I really do miss my mom right now. I think about her long list of nicknames for me in English and Spanish, even the more embarrassing ones like cookie-pie, *gordita*, lu-lu, woo-woo, *pupusa*, honey bunny, *jamoncito* (which means, unbelievably, "little ham"—and I'm a vegetarian!). This is the hardest part of having divorced parents. A lot of the time they're not there when you want them to be. Not at the same time, anyway. Everything gets split up: birthdays, Christmas, other holidays. Half a day here, half a day there. For once, I wish we could be together all day long.

"So what are you going to be for your big party?" Saul asks me.

"I'm not sure yet. Everyone has a costume figured out except me."

CRISTINA GARCÍA

Véronique says she's coming as Edward Scissorhands. (She's had a Johnny Depp fixation for years.) Quincy says he's coming as a mutant frog. Kara promises to come decked out as a biker chick, dressed in leather with lots of makeup and a ripped T-shirt. There's only one problem: no motorcycle. It's not like she can ride in on her brother's scooter. I know she's just trying to impress Eli. She likes him too. Whenever Kara asks him about his costume, he smiles and says, *It's a surprise.*

I still don't have a clue what I'm going to be. Mom read me this funny poem before bed the other night that ended: *I'm just a poor, blind, accordion-playing mouse.* Now *that* would be a good costume.

My Cuban grandparents arrive two days before my party with suitcases filled with more birthday presents for me. Abuela is still behind on my tastes, so there's a bunch of Winnie-the-Pooh items: an address book, a diary, a pen set, and Winnie himself, three feet high and stuffed with fluff. Not to mention a Hello Kitty comforter and matching sheets, complete with uplifted paw. She also bought me several velour sweat suits in neon colors. I glance at my mom as I'm opening the presents, and she gives me a look that says, Keep your mouth shut and say thank you. Politeness is seriously overrated.

Mom has this gift closet where she keeps all the presents she doesn't want and plans to pass on to other people. Half the stuff in there is from Abuela and Gramps. For Christmas last year, they sent Mom this necklace that looked like barbed wire. She still hasn't figured out who to give that to. Finally, I open up a box with pretty T-shirts (hallelujah!), another with embroidered jeans (salvageable), a surfing calendar (very cool), and some flippers (what?!). I'm not sure how my grandparents got the idea that surfers wear flippers, but the image of it makes me laugh out loud.

My grandmother speaks to me in Spanish, which I understand, but I answer her in English. She's always trying to emphasize my Cuban half. To her, being Cuban trumps anything else. It doesn't matter to her who else I am or might like to be. Mom explains that Abuela lost her homeland to the Cuban revolution and it's important for her to keep her identity alive. But what does any of this have to do with me?

Abuela used to get into big arguments with my dad about politics, but now they avoid each other like the plague. Dad says Abuela makes up "facts" to suit whatever argument she is a proponent of at the moment. It's not just big historical events she distorts, but personal ones, too. Like the story of my birth. Everybody has a different take on it, but the one fact that nobody disputes is that Abuela cut my umbilical cord.

My grandmother's version: The head doctor himself asked her to cut it and she dutifully, triumphantly complied.

CRISTINA GARCÍA

My dad's version: Abuela shoved him out of the way and grabbed the scissors from his hands to cut the cord.

My mom's version: Abuela only took the scissors from Dad when he looked like he was about to faint. She said he was deathly pale and his hands were trembling. (My dad vehemently denies this. It's probably one of the reasons they're divorced.)

The night of my party Mom and Abuela get into a pitched battle over whether there should be a prize for best costume.

"What's wrong with being the best?" Abuela shouts. "You want everyone to be treated the same, like they pretend to do in Cuba, but that's not reality. In reality, there's always a winner!" A string of pearls heaves on Abuela's silk blouse. She's wearing a two-piece fuchsia suit with matching pumps. Abuela rubs her pearls like she's trying to conjure up a genie or something.

"But that doesn't mean we have to make everyone else feel like a loser," Mom insists, trying to stay controlled. It reminds me of the way she talks to very little children or how she used to get me to eat my broccoli. "Everybody's worked hard on their costumes. Besides, this is a party we're talking about here. Parties should be fun, remember?"

"I should have never sent you to that liberal college," Abuela spits out. Her eyelids look hooded, like a lizard's.

Mom and Abuela are both more similar and rigid than they realize. They're just on the opposite sides of everything. I sigh and leave the room, thinking it's best to let them fight between themselves.

At the last minute I decide to be a magician for Halloween, and I rush to finish the costume. I twist a bunch of Mom's colorful scarves around my arms and legs and dig up an old top hat she wore to some gender-bender ball years ago. I perch my parakeets on my shoulders but soon have to abandon this because Mango and Peaches start swooping around the house and pooping everywhere. Abuela is freaking out, saying they remind her of the bats that used to fly through Havana at dusk. Bats?! That's a stretch, but I put the birds back in their cage just the same.

Véronique is the first to arrive, and she looks amazing as Edward Scissorhands. She's got this freaky wig on, death mask makeup, and her hands are these huge cardboard and aluminum foil scissors. (She says she borrowed some foil from her huge foil ball to make them.) Her hips look slim and straight as a boy's in black pants and suspenders. Now I regret not having a best costume prize because I'd give it to her straightaway.

Soon the first bunch of people arrive. The costumes are fantastic, and everyone is laughing and pointing at one another and trying to figure out who the Chihuahua is. Mom lit up the backyard, and the pool is glistening in the moonlight like watery lace. There are balloons and streamers and the picnic table is crowded with the best junk food (Mom makes an exception for my birthday): Cheetos, chips and salsa, M&M's, miniature candy bars, homemade chocolate chip cookies, guacamole, boiled soybeans (they're healthy, but I still love them), Dr. Pepper, and Sprite. Later there'll be pizza and ice-cream cake. Everyone starts chasing around the Chihuahua, threatening to unmask him/her, but the Chihuahua is too fast to catch and keeps barking in an annoying, high-pitched kind of way.

At one point Abuela puts on one of my mom's salsa CDs and insists on a costume parade. I'm totally mortified, but everyone gets into it, dancing around the pool in a conga line. Eli is leading it, laughing and shouting, *"Ay, ay, ay, ay, ay"* like he's a deranged mariachi or something—except he's dressed as a lobster, complete with claws and butter sauce. He looks extremely cute. Of course, Kara is right behind him. She opted out of the biker chick idea and came as a baby doll instead, with a short, flouncy dress.

Probably my favorite costume of all is Quincy's. Instead of a mutant frog, he came as the next best thing: a squid! He and Eli—they're good friends—joke that they're a seafood buffet and shout for tartar sauce. They even go up to Abuela and ask her for some in their politest, most earnest voices. She takes them seriously and starts tearing apart the refrigerator to find some. This cracks everyone up even more.

It's only a matter of time before someone ends up in the pool. The first to go in is Lucy Kim, who's dressed as a stalk of asparagus. Second in is the Chihuahua, who turns out to be none other than Michael Gómez, our first violinist. Véronique isn't far behind. Her wig flies off and lands in the deep end of the pool.

It takes three slices of pepperoni pizza and the heroic efforts of Quincy-the-Squid (who retrieves her wig) to settle Véronique down. By then it's a free-for-all and everyone is swimming and chicken fighting even though it's October and cold by L.A. standards. At one point we're lined up by the side of the pool, and on the count of three Quincy shouts: "No peeing in the water!" Then we run and jump in together. It's so much fun, we do it again and again. Mom heated the pool to ninety-two degrees, and she has stacks of towels everywhere so nobody will freeze.

When she turns on the Jacuzzi, that becomes the place to be. Eli puts his arm on my shoulder, leans toward me, and whispers, "Great party." I can feel the wet coolness of his lips against my ear.

This is perfect, I think. I don't want to move. I don't want to get older. I don't want my mom to have a boyfriend. I don't want Saul to die. I want to stop time, right this minute, forever. If only I could keep everything just the way it is: the moon big and full and my friends all around and the last of the summer jasmine perfuming the air like white particles in the dark.

Since practically everyone at my party is a musician, the orchestra problem crops up. There's got to be a way to bring it back. I float the whole fund-raising concert idea again.

"Nobody's gonna pay money to hear us play classical music," Eli groans.

"We've got to show them that we can play other things besides Brahms," I jump in. "How about some rock-'n'-roll?"

"Rock-'n'-roll—us?" Lucy looks skeptical. Her asparagus tip is drooping at a ninety-degree angle off her head.

Quincy convinces us that the entire orchestra should play in the concert, not just a few of the girls, like I suggested online. "This way we'll get the whole school to come!" he shouts, jabbing a tentacle in the air.

We're all stunned for a moment because it seems so obvious and right. Why hadn't we thought of this before? But will people really come? I think about what Saul said: *Go after it like them horses running toward the finish line.* If we sell one thousand tickets—that's only half the seats in the school auditorium—and charge everyone five dollars, we could make enough money to see us through the year.

"How hard can it be?" Quincy is so excited, his tentacles are quivering.

Just then Mom announces she's serving the ice-cream cake, and there's a stampede for the picnic table. Abuela and Gramps start fighting over the digital camera. The singing begins off-key: *"Happy birthday to you! Happy birthday to you! Happy birthday, dear Yumi, happy birthday to you!"* The camera is flashing

(Abuela, no surprise, won the tug-of-war), and my friends are clapping and shouting, "Make a wish! Make a wish!"

There are so many things I want to wish for, but none of them seem as important as having Saul. *Please, please let Saul live a little longer. I know he's ninety-two and nobody lives forever but I wish—okay, this is official—I wish he can live long enough to see our concert.* Then I take a deep breath, so deep it makes my lungs ache, and I blow out the candles: thirteen of them, plus one for good luck.

Hey, Yumi girl! It's good to see you, kid. What do you have for me there? You saved me a piece of your birthday cake? Now don't let your grandmother see it, heh-heh. You know I could never say no to a little cake, especially yours. Why don't you play me some music while I eat, eh? So how's the orchestra campaign going? Oh yeah? Count me in, little one. I'll be in the first row. So what are you going to play for me? A new piece? Okay, I'll sit back and listen. . . . That's just beautiful, Yumi girl. You got some serious talent there. Yeah, kid, mark my words. You're gonna be the next Benny Goodman.

You want me to keep going with the story? You don't give up, do you? That's a good thing. Before you know it, you'll be my age, telling your own granddaughter the story of your life. And you wanna make it an interesting one, don't you? You wanna be able to tell her some adventures, some excitement, some something. How you live your life, little one, is a gift for those who come after

CRISTINA GARCÍA

you. A kind of inheritance. I can't leave you no money—no fancy house or nothing like that—but I can leave you my experiences. And maybe you can learn a little something from them.

Well, the people of my time have passed on, Yumi girl. Look at me. I'm the last one alive in my family by twenty years. Nobody's ready for death. If you ask Joe Blow on the street, he ain't gonna tell you he thinks he'll live forever. But when the end is near, you realize you've been believing that all along. It's like getting caught with your pants down. That's why you gotta live, little one. Yeah, stop and smell them roses. Take advantage of everything your parents are doing for you. Look how you get to travel around the world with your mother. How many kids your age been riding on an elephant in Vietnam?

Okay, I'll get back to my story. I'd been wanting to tell you about the Depression and realized there ain't nobody I know from those years still around. Those were hard times, kid. People lost everything they had. Families were turned out of their homes for not paying the rent. There was no work. Prohibition was over, but there were still lots of clubs—"speakeasies" we called them—in the back alleys of New York and Chicago. People could drink and dance and forget their troubles. Some of the best bands of the times got started in them.

Those clubs had some serious gambling in the back rooms. Poker, mostly. You had to know somebody to get in a game. You couldn't just walk in off the street, you know what I'm saying? Well, it turned out I wasn't too bad at poker, neither. Mind you, I didn't get rich or nothing, but I made enough to get by. Yeah, I did all right. I was living in a hotel then. I had my room, my meals, my laundry done and delivered overnight. What more did I need?

It took many a down-and-out year before the country got back on its feet. I gotta hand it to FDR, he did everything he could. Franklin Delano Roosevelt. Greatest president who ever lived. Don't let nobody tell you different. But I hate to say it was World War II that really got the country moving again. War means jobs, screwed up as that is. Years later President Eisenhower—a general himself, mind you—called it the "military-industrial complex." And that's the honest truth of it. There's money to be made in conflict, kid. Ain't that why lawyers are so rich? I tried to get your dad to go to law school, but he wouldn't hear of it. He could do his music on the side, I told him, like a hobby. But your dad didn't pay me no mind.

What are you studying in history, Yumi? Ancient Mesopotamia? So you haven't gotten to World War II yet? Your mother's told you about it? Good, good. You should know these things. In the late 1930s news trickled out of Europe about what the Germans were doing to the Jews, but nobody believed it. Who could imagine such a thing? I'm a Jew myself and I didn't believe it. No, I didn't have no family there. My mother came to America when she was a girl. Her family was from Minsk, in Russia. My father's family, too. They got sick of the pogroms and whatnot and decided to come to America.

Pearl Harbor changed everything. December 7, 1941. "A day

that will live in infamy." That's what FDR said. And he was right. Suddenly, the war was in our own backyard. You should've seen people getting riled up about it. Before you know it, the government started rounding up the Japanese Americans and putting them in internment camps. A disgrace, if there ever was one. Two months after Pearl Harbor, I got drafted. Twenty-eight years old—did I mention how good-looking I was? Heh-heh. It was off to the army for me. I gotta tell you it was the biggest shock of my life.

I did my basic training at Fort Dix. I'd never run around the block, much less ten miles with a heavy backpack. At night my head would hit the pillow and bam!—I was out cold. It felt like two minutes later they were blowing the bugle to wake us up. I was always the last one out of my bunk. "Get up, Wise Guy!" the sergeant shouted at me in the morning. If I wasn't fast enough, he'd pour a bucketful of ice on me. Son of a gun! You should've seen me move my tuchas then!

Everyone called me "Wise Guy" because I was from Brooklyn and I made them laugh. That's what saved me from those mean, corn-fed Kansas boys. That and the fact that I ran a few numbers games on the side. Made myself some extra change. By the way, here's your dollar for the week. Don't spend it all in one place, heh-heh.

So where does Uncle Sam send me after nearly killing me in boot camp? The Pacific Theater. Made it sound like I was heading into some action movie with John Wayne. But I ended up in Alaska. The Aleutian Islands, to be specific. Think about what the middle *of nowhere means to you. No houses, no people, just ice and water and blue-gray skies as far as the eye can see.*

Now think that because you're so far up north, winter daylight lasts maybe three hours tops. And that it's so cold, the tears in your eyeballs freeze up. And that the sight of anything colorful—an apple, a scarf—looks bright enough to blind you. That was Alaska. Four years I spent there, mostly driving the generals around. Yeah, I was a chauffeur. Why can't I drive now? I never got no license. New Yorkers ain't a driving bunch. Ask your mother, she'll tell you. Just the same, I rose to corporal. Corporal of ice and jeeps, that was me.

The biggest excitement my whole time there was when Ingrid Bergman came to visit. She was the most beautiful actress who ever lived, if you ask me. Who knows what she was doing in Alaska, but I got to drive her around for a whole morning. Kept me warm for a year, believe me. A gorgeous woman, that Ingrid Bergman. The most gorgeous woman I ever seen except for your grandmother. Wait a minute, let me say that a little louder: THE MOST GORGEOUS WOMAN I EVER SEEN EXCEPT FOR YOUR GRANDMOTHER! There, that should get me a steak dinner.

The moose? Ah, the moose happened on account of us getting cabin fever. You see, we got time off, but we had nowhere to go. It wasn't like we could fly to San Francisco and back in a weekend. So some of the guys got this cockamamie idea to go camping—anything to get off the base. Nearly froze to death and

CRISTINA GARCÍA

it was springtime. In the middle of our first night out, I'm needing to go the bathroom real bad. So I'm out in the woods when I hear this crashing sound behind me. I figure it's one of the guys—Tony Perotta was the practical joker—so I zip up my pants, turn around, and come face-to-face with the biggest moose I ever seen. The thing must've been nine feet tall! Gigantic nostrils with steam coming out of them.

Well, I started running faster than I ever did in my life! I didn't dare turn around, but I could hear that moose galloping behind me, antlers and all. You think them animals are so huge they can't run, but that moose must've been going thirty miles an hour. I'm telling you, Yumi, I was going at least thirty-five! Somebody should've clocked me. I was the fastest man alive on the planet that instant, believe me. Just when I couldn't hold out any longer, I spotted a big pine tree and climbed it, I don't know how. The moose finally got bored and drifted away, chewing something or other. It took me all night to get the pine needles out of places you don't even want to hear about. Yeah, yeah, it may sound funny now, but I was scared witless.

A WEEK AFTER MY PARTY MOM STARTS PACKING UP THE
house. She says that we're moving out at the end of
December, that she's sublet an apartment a few miles away
for the rest of the school year. She's applied for one last
teaching job in Los Angeles. If she gets it, we stay in L.A.
If she doesn't, we move up to Napa, where Mom has that
house she's been renting out for years. We lived there the
summer before I started first grade. I still remember it. The
day we moved in, I fell off a ladder and Mom had to rush me
to the emergency room. I fractured my left baby toe. It still
looks nothing like the rest of my foot—an alien reminder of
where I don't belong.

I love my house now, the one I'm about to lose. We've
been living in it for seven years, even though Mom says

it's never really been ours. It's a two-story, Spanish-style house with a pool and enormous windows that overlook the Pacific Ocean. Practically every room has a view, even my mom's closet and my playroom. The rent started out pretty reasonable, but definitely it's an "as is" situation. The roof leaks, the plumbing is ancient, and last year we had an infestation of rats in the attic (*Third World living at its best*, Mom joked). But it's the only place I've ever called home. How could we be moving?

I learned how to swim here, and I get to see the ocean every single day. Sometimes Mom will wake me up in the morning shouting: *Dolphin alert!* I rush to my window and climb out onto the balcony to watch a school of dolphins maybe twenty yards offshore. I stand there mesmerized until I can't see them anymore. Once I saw a mother and baby dolphin together. I think the baby was just learning how to jump because it kept flailing into the air every few minutes. It was so sweet! And at night the sound of the ocean is the last thing I hear before falling asleep.

How can we leave all this? If it weren't for my living in this house, I might've never picked up surfing either. Mom says I can surf in northern California, too, but it turns out that there are more shark attacks there than any other place in the world. In fact, the great white sharks breed and feed in what's known as the Red Triangle. Mom blanched when I told her this, but then she reassured me that we'd find safe places.

It doesn't help that Mom is stressed about everything lately. She's acting like the big martyr these days, griping about how nobody helps out with anything, that she's a struggling single mother, that she can't concentrate on her writing with all the lecturing and packing and cleaning she's doing. I've never heard her complain so much. She's taken to drinking herbal teas with names like Serenity, Zen, Chai, Calm. But I think someone switched the labels at the health food store and what she's actually drinking is Extra Annoying.

"You need to learn to bloom where you're planted," Mom tells me on the third day of packing. She's trying to put a good spin on things.

"I'm already blooming where I'm planted," I shoot back. "You know, most plants die when you transplant them."

"Not if you do it carefully," Mom snaps. "Besides, now you'll have a chance to reinvent yourself."

"What's wrong with the me I already am?" I'm about to lose it, and my eyeballs hurt from trying not to cry.

"Nothing, *mi amor*," she says in a more conciliatory tone. "Just that you'll have opportunities to expand your horizons. You can become anyone you want to be."

"But I *like* who I am!" I shout.

Later in my room I think some more about what Mom said. I do kind of like the idea of coming up with a whole new me, theoretically at least. I dedicate the back portion of my geometry notebook to short bios on the new Yumi Ruíz-

Hirsch, like the ones that appear on the jacket flaps of my mom's books. Here's a sampler:

> YUMI RUÍZ-HIRSCH was surfing before she could walk and has taken on the biggest, baddest waves on the planet. Ms. Ruíz-Hirsch is the official spokesperson for Cowabunga Unlimited and recently started her own magazine, *Surfer Chick (Not)*, for serious female surfers. She plans to attend UC Santa Cruz.

> YUMI RUÍZ-HIRSCH is a world-famous trainer of English bulldogs. Although the breed is notorious for its sloth, Ms. Ruíz-Hirsch has managed to coax the dogs to do the impossible: walk tightropes, bring slippers, flush the toilet. Her new book, *Millie and Me*, will be published next year by Bowwow Press.

> YUMI RUÍZ-HIRSCH is a clarinetist with the Berlin Philharmonic, the youngest musician and first female admitted to the orchestra. She's also performed as a guest soloist with the New York,

Philadelphia, and Chicago symphonies, as well as with London's punk legends. She is fluent in Spanish and German.

YUMI RUÍZ-HIRSCH started baking cookies in her mother's kitchen at the age of four. By second grade her chocolate chip varieties were outselling the Girl Scouts of Greater Los Angeles. Today Ms. Ruíz-Hirsch oversees her baking empire, Cookies for Humanity, from her seaside home in Southern California, the same one she grew up in.

YUMI RUÍZ-HIRSCH is a writer and filmmaker whose works have been shown at festivals worldwide. Her latest film, *Into the Dark Hour,* a documentary about nighttime surfing, was nominated for an Academy Award and won her a MacArthur "Genius" Fellowship at age thirteen.

Well okay, you get the idea.

When I tell Véronique about the move, she totally freaks out and starts running in circles around my bedroom. It's Friday night, and we're having a sleepover at my house.

"You can't, Yooms, you just can't move away!" she cries, already breathless after a few laps. "We're best friends. Best friends don't move away. That's impossible."

"It's not a hundred percent sure yet. My mom is applying for a job here, so we still might stay."

"Yeah, but your house! You're moving out of the perfect house. *Our* perfect house. How can someone else live here? We won't let them!" The pressure—not to mention the aerobics—is too much for Véronique, and she collapses to the floor. "No, it can't be true!" she wails.

I want to cry too, but I try to keep it together. "It'll be okay, don't worry. We'll always be best friends, no matter what." I wish I could sound more cheery, but I'm not feeling it. I look around my bedroom. How many days and nights have we spent here giggling and telling each other secrets? Even our bedtime stuffed animals lie side by side on my bed.

Hers: Dodo-dog, shredded beyond recognition into a brown pulp, with the remains of a baby blanket tied around its head.

Mine: Lena, a plaid cow my dad gave me when I was two. Hiroko has patched and resewn her so many times, it's hard to tell what's original. But it's partly out of respect for Lena that I don't eat meat.

All my memories are stored in this house. I learned how to bake chocolate chip cookies and poppy seed cake and oven fries here with my mom. I've read all my favorite books here. I played with our bulldogs in this very living room. And my parakeets have been parked at my bedroom window for five years. We spent every Christmas I can remember here. I can't imagine not having any of this anymore. I don't want to move away. I don't want to move to Pacific Palisades, or Napa, or anywhere that isn't here.

Véronique has settled into her sniffling stage, and I know the conversation will soon turn to her favorite topic: boys. I blame all the romance novels she reads—books with heroines whose bustlines are bigger than their IQs. But Véronique believes the books give her insight into romantic love, and she quotes them while dissecting the latest gossip at school. She has a crush on Nick Francisco, another double bassist, who she insists looks just like Johnny Depp (he doesn't).

"Guess what?" I say, heading her off at the pass. "My mom saw Laird Hamilton at the gym!"

"No way! Did she get his autograph?"

"Nah, I'm so mad at her."

"My mom never sees anyone," Véronique complains. "What's more boring than spending the whole day doing accounting?"

"At least she's not trying to move or having boyfriends."

"God, I can't even imagine that! That would be seriously weird."

"Tell me about it. Jim is coming to visit for Thanksgiving, and I'm supposed to be nice to him. There's nothing worse than seeing them all lovey-dovey. There should be a law against public displays of affection for anyone over thirty, period."

"I want to meet him," Véronique says. "See if he's good enough for you and your mom."

"Look, Millie already slobbers over him. It's like he wants to take over my whole family. I don't want you to like him too!"

"Is he that awful?"

"It would be a lot easier if he were. But no, he's just average. Average height. Average looks. Average everything. I've never heard him say anything even remotely interesting or funny. What's Mom doing with him, anyway?"

Talking about Jim makes me sad—sad for me and sad for my dad, too.

Then, to get our minds off the subject, Véronique suggests we watch a movie—with Johnny Depp in it, of course. Somewhere in the middle of our forty-seventh viewing of *Edward Scissorhands*, we fall asleep.

It's the Sunday before Thanksgiving, and most of the orchestra is packed into my enormous, half-empty living room. The first rehearsal isn't going well. First of all, there are way too many of us. Fifty-seven altogether. But I don't have the heart to cut anybody.

A week ago we officially launched the Bring Back Our

Orchestra Now! campaign. Quincy and I were voted co-chairs of the whole operation. We've been spending hours at school and on the phone getting this thing off the ground. So far we've circulated a petition, sold treble-clef-shaped cookies at lunchtime, and staged a protest outside the principal's office. Quincy tried to get a reporter from a local cable station to come down and interview us after school, but she never showed.

When word gets around that we're going to put on a fund-raising concert, that the orchestra will actually be playing punk, everyone wants to join in. People who aren't in the orchestra or don't even play an instrument are coming around. Since my dad's in a band, Quincy lets me decide on the first couple of songs to try. I figure if we can work out a few killer tunes, we might have a chance at putting on a decent performance—or at least not making total fools of ourselves. We're shooting for a Valentine's Day concert.

Instead of concentrating on the music, everyone is fighting over what to wear and who should replace the percussionist who moved to Vancouver.

"I think we should be in concert dress to maintain a little dignity," Lucy insists. "I mean, who are we trying to kid?"

"Forget that!" Quincy argues. "Let's all wear bowling shirts with our own logo!"

This starts another fight about what the logo should be.

"Why don't we just wear sunglasses on stage?" Kara suggests. "They're cheap and they're cool—"

"And they'll prevent us from reading our music," Quincy interrupts. "Maybe that's a *good* thing!"

The doorbell rings, and it's Véronique, carrying her violin case and a paper bag. "I heard we need a percussionist?" She pulls a pair of toy-store maracas from the bag, and everyone laughs.

"People, people!" I shout, trying to restore some order. "Let's take it from the top, please!"

I've picked out "White Riot" by the Clash, a band many of them have never heard of, and "Anarchy in the U.K." by the Sex Pistols. Dad suggested I punk up a good reggae song too, so I've included Bob Marley's "One Love." We got Zoë's uncle, a music professor, to arrange everything for the orchestra. How tough can this be? My friends are used to playing much more technically difficult pieces. But I'm learning this lesson fast: The simpler the song, the tougher it is to pull off.

The first run-through sounds like we're strangling farm animals with our bare hands. There are no adjectives for this. My parakeets are going bonkers upstairs, screeching and chirping as if they might be next. Maybe French horns and violas were never meant to play rock-'n'-roll. What was I thinking?

"Okay, everyone," I shout again, clapping my hands and feeling like a total imposter. Nobody is listening to me. "Let's take it from the top. Remember, there is no adagio here. The closest thing would be a combination of *pesante* with *allegro con fuoco.* Ready? Think hard, think fast, think: *Take no prisoners!*" Eli makes an obscene sound with his tuba (it's kind of a specialty with him), and everyone cracks up.

To my surprise, Quincy comes to my defense. "Listen up, you guys! Whoever doesn't want to do this can just leave right now. Yumi isn't messing around. We've got a show to put on, with or without you."

I shoot Squid-boy a brief, grateful smile, and he smiles back, his double bass poised to play. Eli looks at him, then back at me. Mom traipses in with a tray of hot chocolates and bowls of 94 percent fat-free popcorn. (At least she isn't offering her mushroom-stuffed endive this time.) I can tell she's worried—whether it's over me or the chances of the neighbors calling the police, I'm not sure.

After she delivers the snacks, Mom makes a semidiscreet phone call. A half hour later, just when I'm ready to throw up my hands in disgust, my dad appears. He takes over the rehearsal like a drill sergeant, barking orders and rearranging the instrumentation like a pro. I've never seen him so focused, like he's come out of his stupor.

"Ladies and gentlemen," he announces before our final run-through, "this is war. This is for anybody who's ever trashed you or made you feel small. This is for the teachers who can't spell 'omniscient.' This is for the parents who keep you leashed up like you can't be trusted. This is for the narrow-minded, ignorant, classist, xenophobic idiots who presume to tell you how to live. Play like you can convince them. Play like the giants you are!"

For a moment everyone just stares at my dad with their mouths open. I can only imagine what they're thinking. *Is that really Yumi's father? Where did they find this guy? Why doesn't my dad ever say stuff like that?* Then, on a fast count of eight, we begin. It feels like we're playing in this big wind tunnel, giving it all we've got. The sound comes together in an amazing way. I'm playing my clarinet like it's on fire, and I see everyone around me doing the same. The bass section is arched back, the bells of their instruments aimed at the ceiling. The flute players' eyes are bugged out from playing so hard. Even the violinists have never looked more intense. We're deep inside the music, playing it straight from our hearts.

Wow. I wish we could've recorded ourselves. By the time we get to the end of Bob Marley's rocking-fast, punked-out "One Love," we sit there in a state of shock. It's one of those forever, dragged-out moments, but in the best kind of way. Then we raise our clarinets, our bassoons, our French horns, our trombones, and the bows of our string instruments and cheer for all we're worth.

Thanksgiving is a real comedown after the orchestra rehearsal. In fact, the whole week heads downhill fast. Dad sinks back into his depression. Mom is in overdrive, trying to make every-thing perfect for the holiday. She wanted to make a roast pork instead of a turkey for Thanksgiving, but everyone told her it was sacrilegious, including me, and I don't eat either one. So instead, she treated the turkey as if it were pork, marinating it Cuban style for three days with tons of garlic, cumin, oregano, onions, and sour oranges.

Mom also prepared enough black beans, rice, fried plantains, yucca in garlic sauce (yes, more garlic!), and avocado-and-onion salad for an army—make that two armies. After a meal like this, we could probably take Canada or something.

So we're finally sitting around the Thanksgiving table making small talk. Mom claims there's nothing she hates more than mindless chatter, but she's all ears listening to Jim get windbaggy about a hailstorm in Texas that dented his car in seventy-two places. Like he's inventoried every ding? "The land is so flat, you can see thunderstorms coming a hundred miles off," Jim says, all serious. "I just open the curtains wide and watch them like they're theater."

I'm thinking: *Does anyone in the world besides meteorologists find this the least bit interesting? Besides, isn't he an orchestra conductor? Why is he talking about the weather? And why does he keep touching my mother's hand? It's really getting on my nerves.*

Mom has invited two of her closest friends over to check him out—I overheard her telling them that she has terrible taste in men (does this include my dad?). It's hard to say how things are going by adult standards. I'm bored out of my mind and start balancing plantains on my fork, fantasizing about launching them in Jim's direction. Smack! Right to the forehead. I imagine the grease streaking his aviator glasses from another century. They're so retro, they're borderline cool.

Jim brought me a present: a neck strap to take the pressure off my thumb when I play the clarinet. It's a thoughtful gift—I know, I know—but isn't that like giving somebody a toaster? He says he's eager to hear me play again, but that's the last thing I want to do. Last time he was here, Jim made a few suggestions about my playing. He told me how to support my breath better, that I needed to try for a more even tone in the higher registers. Nothing my own teacher hasn't told me, except *he isn't my teacher!* Besides, he plays the *cello*. What does he really know about the clarinet? Even if he does conduct the Texas Youth Symphony, he has no right to give me unsolicited advice.

I think Mom is hoping I'll ask him for help with our Bring Back the Orchestra Now! campaign. Let's just say she shouldn't hold her breath on that one.

Dad's at the table with us, and he's on his fourth glass of wine. "Garlic," he repeats for the tenth time, "upsets my stomach." Then he leans over to me and whispers: "Your mother sabotaged Thanksgiving dinner just for me." If he only knew how little she thinks about him, it would make him feel even worse. Out of nowhere, Dad clinks his glass with his knife to get everyone's attention and decides to tell a joke.

"So a gang of snails attacks a tree sloth and steals his wallet," he begins, slurring his words slightly. "Down at the station the police chief questions the sloth. 'So how'd they get you, sir?' The sloth turns his head slowly and says: 'Darned if I know, it happened so fast.'" Dad breaks up laughing, like he's just heard the funniest thing in the world.

Everyone but him looks mortified. Millie trundles by looking for a handout, and he gives her a garlicky turkey leg and a pat on the head. She burps loudly in gratitude.

Mom glares at Dad, then turns, smiling, to her Nigerian writer friend. Sonny is a big guy with an unexpectedly gentle voice. Mom thinks he's a genius. He tells a long story about the plague of locusts that denuded the trees of his village when he was a boy. Jim looks ashamed about his dumb, hail-dented car after that. Simone, my mother's nuts-and-leafy-greens-eating friend, talks about last year's tsunami in Asia. To drown, to have her breathing impeded in any way, she says, is her greatest fear. She's working through this in yoga. The conversation takes a turn toward natural disasters: earthquakes, volcano eruptions, the record number of hurricanes this season. Is global warming to blame? The melting ice caps? The use of aerosol deodorants?

I try to think of my own worst fear. Is one way of dying better than another? Getting caught in a burning building? Having an elevator fall with me inside it? Plunging to my death over a cliff? Would it be worse to know you were going to die ahead of time? Or better if death caught you by surprise? I think of Saul living with the knowledge that he's going to die soon. Why isn't he climbing the Himalayas or signing up for one of those space shuttles to Mars? But Saul tells me the highlight of his week is when I visit him. He says that's what keeps him hanging on. That and his nightly cigar.

Jim takes the moment of uncomfortable silence following the disaster talk to stand up and make a toast to my mother: "To my beautiful, beautiful Silvia, the love of my life." I feel my stomach churning. Dad notices me and squeezes my hand, as if to say, *I know just how you feel.* Then, in front of everyone, Jim gets down on one knee and takes Mom's hands in his (she has to wipe some garlic sauce off first). He offers her a tiny velvet box with an engagement ring inside. *Oh no! Say no, quick! Before it's too late!* I want to shout this as loud as I can, but I'm struck dumb.

The ring seems to grow in slow motion before my eyes. It's a big diamond with triangles of sapphires on either side. It sparkles so much, I feel blinded, a blindness you might get from staring at an eclipse of the sun. I catch a glimpse of Mom, and she's looking melty-gooey-gaga and her skin is a deep shade of pink. She's embarrassed and excited at the same time. Jim clears his throat and asks Mom to marry him, just like that. And to my complete and utter horror, she looks at him lovingly and says yes.

ᦉᦉ

So your mother's getting married, eh? Hope springs eternal et cetera, et cetera. Your dad was there when he proposed? How'd he take it? What? He told a joke about a sloth? Tell it to me. . . . Heh-heh, I gotta remember that one. Well, I don't know what to tell you, Yumi. Your parents split up a long time ago. Nobody told us nothing. From one day to the next, it just happened. Me and Hiroko racked our brains trying to figure out what went wrong. But who really knows what tears people apart? No, I'm sure it had nothing to do with you, little one.

It's a good thing Hiroko's at the supermarket. Don't tell her nothing yet. She's got enough on her plate. Last couple of days I've been feeling weak. Hardly got out of bed except to read the paper. Hiroko's been pushing me to do chemotherapy, but I told her over my dead body. Look here, I'm ninety-two years old. I ain't a spring chicken no more. Maybe I should've eaten yogurt like those old farts in them commercials. But nobody lives forever, not even them.

I remember when your parents got married. They were living in Hawaii that year. Your mother was doing some kind of fellowship there, and your dad went along for the ride. That was his problem right off. It ain't a good idea to follow nobody around. The two of them had this bungalow on Oahu that looked out over a bay—it was a swamp, really, but Silvia insisted on calling it a bay, and you don't argue with her, if you know what I mean. That's where they had the wedding. Rained like the dickens, but in Hawaii that's supposed to bring good luck.

Anyway, back to my story. Three months after World War II was over, I was discharged at Niagara Falls and made my way back to New York City. I started hearing a lot of stories from soldiers who'd been stationed in Japan and the Philippines. I told myself I had to do something with my life. I didn't want to be sitting around some veterans' hall boasting about the adventures I never had. Anyway, long story to say that I tossed a coin: Heads, I go to China; tails, I go to Japan. Well, you know how it turned out.

Nearly every cent of my discharge pay went to buying the plane ticket to Tokyo. I thought I'd never get there. Longest flight I ever took. The plane stopped in San Francisco, then Honolulu, before finally landing in Japan. I couldn't believe my eyes when I got there. The Depression was nothing compared to this. The country was on its knees. And I didn't go near Hiroshima or Nagasaki neither. That's where we dropped them atom bombs, kid. It was so horrible that nobody has dropped another one since.

By hook and by crook, I ended up working for the port of Yokohama. Remember how I liked the Brooklyn docks as a kid? Well, I knew it was where I belonged. Soon enough they put me in charge of importing automobiles and machine parts, anything to get the country running again. They needed someone who spoke English and could deal with the big American contractors. That's how war works, little one. First we destroy a country, then we make money building it up again. My Japanese wasn't too bad in those days neither.

So, before you know it, I'm running the whole port. I got the

CRISTINA GARCÍA

Japanese what they needed, and I made the Americans happy, and I got paid a lot of money for doing it, too. Not everyone understood both cultures like I did. Yeah, people liked and respected me on both sides. I got things done and was as good as my word. Don't make promises you can't keep, kid. But keep the ones you do make. That's how people will learn to trust you, how you build up confidence in yourself.

In those days I was living in the best hotel in Yokohama. People chased after me: "Yes, Mr. Hirsch. Right away, Mr. Hirsch. Whatever you say, Mr. Hirsch." For the first time in my life I was a big shot. I gotta admit I loved it, maybe too much. But it was a lot better than being a nobody. I liked to peel off a hundred-dollar bill for a two-dollar steak dinner and watch the waiter scramble around for change. Then I'd leave the guy a twenty-dollar tip. Next time I show up, my name is golden.

Things were good for a long time, kid. I spent the best fifteen years of my life in Japan. Even destroyed as the country was, you couldn't take away its beauty. The mountains—I wish we could go to Mount Fuji, little one. And there's no place more beautiful than Japan in the spring. They go nuts over them cherry blossoms. You'd think every tree was visiting royalty.

Little by little, Japan picked itself up, dusted itself off, and started all over again—just like the song goes. Factories up and running, roads rebuilt, the fishermen out in their boats, the markets teeming with vegetables and whatnot. And I was glad to do my part. The Japanese are the hardest-working people on earth. *If you don't believe me, look at your grandmother. I don't think I've ever seen the woman sleep!*

I'd do it all over again in a heartbeat, Yumi girl. That's what I tell your father: Live a little, get out, have some fun. What's he moping around for? Nobody's gonna make your destiny for you. You gotta go out and make it for yourself. Take a few risks. Austin is forty-four years old, tuning pianos, playing his music for a bunch of nobodies. When's he gonna join the dance?

Sometimes I think of that turtle he had as a kid. Your father loved that turtle, called him Arthur. Well, Arthur hid under a log in his aquarium all day long. Your father would make up adventures for him, but the fact was, that turtle didn't do nothing. You ever hear the expression "a bump on a log"? I don't want you ending up like some turtle hiding under a log. You hear me?

You keep asking me how I met Hiroko, and I want to tell you. Now, she'll probably contradict everything I say, but there's at least two sides to every story. Don't let nobody tell you different. Hiroko was nineteen years old, scrawny and dressed plain as a peasant, but I could tell there was a real beauty about her. She had a noodle stand outside the American naval base in Yokohama. Yeah, she parked herself right outside the front gates. The MPs told her to get lost every day for a month, but she kept coming back, and pretty soon she had everyone—from the admirals on down—hooked on her noodles with beef.

Nobody could come by much beef in Japan then, but Hiroko found a way. She knew the Americans weren't going to be satisfied with tiny bits of chicken they had to find with a magnifying glass. Nothing but grade A beef would do for them. Somehow, Hiroko managed to get it. She kept her distance from the sailors too, which I liked. Never wore no makeup, never flirted with them, dressed in those shapeless farmer pants. She was friendly but formal, if you know what I mean. She had no time for malingerers.

Let's just say I had my eye on the girl. Watched her from a distance for weeks before I bought a bowl of her noodles. You gotta remember I was eating in the fanciest places—foreign hotels, the officers' club. I wore tailor-made suits, everything silk down to my drawers. Nothing but the best. I wouldn't buy no noodles from just anyone, you hear me? But something about her caught my attention. Maybe it was her hands, small and strong and delicate, like my mother's.

That Hiroko was a tough cookie. Didn't give me the time of day for three months. Took me another three before she let me take her to a baseball game. Your grandmother was a fanatic. Knew her statistics like nobody's business. She said something that's impressed me to this day: "The pitcher's job is to make the batter understand too late." Heh-heh. It's still the best definition of a pitcher I ever heard.

For the first time in years I found myself courting a woman. Dinners, flowers, little gifts. To my surprise, I liked it. If truth be told, kid, I fell in love with her. And I think she fell in love with me. Everyone looked at us and figured that Hiroko was dating me for my money. But I'm telling you, the money didn't figure into it.

Why would she still be with me today? I knew I wanted to marry her when I started thinking of what our child would look like. Yeah, I wanted a girl. A girl don't judge you so harshly as a boy. But I had to wait a long time until you came along, little one.

5 DECEMBER

IT'S A WEEK BEFORE CHRISTMAS, AND I'M SITTING IN THIS FANCY hotel in Guatemala City. We're here picking up my aunt's new baby, my one and only cousin-to-be. Right after Thanksgiving, Tía Paloma called my mom in the middle of the night. "I found her!" she announced. Mom raced to the computer and saw her: a brown speck of a girl they instantly named Isabel. Suddenly, it was Isabel this and Isabel that. Three weeks later we're all in Guatemala trying to bring her home. It's not as easy as you might think. My aunt figured she could just swoop down here, sign the paperwork, and rush back to Brooklyn with the baby in time for Christmas. Now it looks like it'll be months before Tía Paloma can take Isabel home. The government is deciding whether to change its adoption rules, and everything is in limbo.

Okay, I'll admit this right up front: I've never been a big baby fan. I like dogs a whole lot more. But little Isabel is growing on me. Our first two days (this is our fourth) were a complete nightmare. Isabel cried and cried and cried. And whenever she pooped, I fled the scene of the crime. We're talking *seriously* toxic. Mom says it stinks so bad because they've changed formulas to one with more iron and vitamins. Whatever the reason, it's deadly.

My mom immediately took charge of the baby—changing her diapers, giving her birdbaths in the sink, freshening her up with talcum powder, arranging her hair into funny-looking pompadours that make her look like a tiny Elvis. Slowly, I came around and started hanging out with Isabel more. She's four and a half months old and has the tiniest lips and fingernails. Today I played part of a Mozart concerto for her on my clarinet. Isabel got all happy and started waving her arms and kicking her legs. Then just before I was finished, she sank into a deep sleep.

"Everyone's a critic," Mom laughed.

My mother bought a digital video camera for the trip, but she's hopeless with anything technological, so she put me in charge of doing the movies. I can't believe how much fun it is. I conduct these mock interviews with Isabel, where I ask her questions and interpret her gurgles and cooing for the camera. Q: *So, Isabel, do you think you'll be more of a chocolate person or a vanilla person? A: Gooo, gaaaa-ahhhh. (Okay, that was definitely vanilla!) Or: Tell us what your favorite color is,*

Isabel. *Do you have one yet?* A: *Eeeeeeeeooooooo. (That sounds like green to me! Moving right along . . .)* What I especially like is taking shots at odd angles, like a close-up of Isabel's armpit or her big toe, which wriggles when I touch it. I told Mom I'm definitely keeping the camera when we get back to L.A.

The hotel we're staying in is super deluxe, and we have a working television set—a first for me as far as my mom is concerned. Mostly, it shows weird game shows with contestants decked out in evening gowns. Sometimes I get to see old American movies dubbed in Spanish. Last night when Isabel was cranky, I watched *American Graffiti*. They gave the Ron Howard character this deep macho voice, which was hilarious.

There are dozens of security guards at the hotel. When I ask my mom why, she goes into a long diatribe about the country's plantation society, how the rich landowners and military massacred the indigenous peoples, how the civil war claimed two hundred thousand lives, how innocent children were caught in the cross fire between the army and the guerrillas. Students, labor leaders, innocent peasants—nobody was spared.

Mom is agitated because there's some kind of military conference going on at the hotel. The elevators open, and we're suddenly face-to-face with a row of Latin American generals. It's all Mom can do to keep her mouth shut. And sometimes she doesn't even do that. Yesterday she overheard an Argentine accent in the lobby and went right up to the major, or whatever he was, and demanded to know about the fate of the *desaparecidos*, the people who the army made "disappear." He looked at her like she was from another planet.

None of us are supposed to leave the hotel with the baby except for prearranged appointments to the doctor's office. It's one of a long list of rules the Guatemalan lawyer gave us when we arrived. Mom wants to get out and see the country, but she's afraid to leave her sister alone with Isabel for long. We went to the market downtown for a couple of hours yesterday. Mom was in her element, charging up and down the aisles, bargaining over things she didn't even want.

What Mom bought: three cotton dresses for Isabel, a brightly colored woven tablecloth, a hand-painted plate, a salad bowl, a jaguar mask, three expensive guayaberas for Jim, and a cheap blue one for my dad.

What I bought: a package of gum and an orange soda.

I couldn't wait to get back to the hotel. The market was crowded and dirty, and a whole section of it sold live animals: chickens and piglets and songbirds in twig cages. It made me sad to look at them. Kids my age and younger were staring at me—most of them were *working* there—and it made me self-conscious. Mom thinks it's good for me to be exposed to the way other people live so I won't take my privileges for granted. But if she wanted me to feel guilty about the way we live, why do we live the way we do in the first place? And why does she bargain so hard with people much poorer than us? Shouldn't she be giving them money instead?

While she's doing the market tango with some toothless guy (she claims she can flirt her way down to a better price with the male vendors), I try to imagine it snowing in Guatemala. A pristine snow that would cover everything in a glistening white blanket: the cathedral, and the marketplace, and the taxicabs, and the men selling ice cream and soft drinks from their little tinkling carts. I imagine filming a movie of Guatemala City slowly surrendering to the snow. Well, maybe just for an hour or so. I wouldn't want anyone freezing to death.

It's Sunday and we're sitting around the pool with the other adoptive mothers. Everyone has a story to tell. I'm looking at this flat-headed baby who mostly stares into space. His mother-to-be is a middle-aged tomboy who trains horses in New Jersey. There's also a lesbian couple adopting three brothers, all under five. Mom says it's wonderful that the boys will stay together. I get to thinking about accidents of birth, how families are made in so many ways. Take my mother and her sister, for example. They were born within a year of each other and though they have a few similarities, they're very different. Was it luck or destiny that they ended up sisters?

I like my aunt, but she's high-strung. As an elementary school principal, she's used to having things done her way. The Guatemalan lawyer is promising her the moon, saying the government will decide on her case soon, but nothing is happening. It's making Tía Paloma crazy. She and my mom talk a lot alike—they have identical voices and call each other "doll face" in thick Brooklyn accents. But they don't look anything alike and don't talk about the same things. For Mom, no subject is taboo. My girlfriends will ask her things they're too afraid to ask their own mothers. Tía Paloma, on the other hand, is touchy about a lot of stuff. *Certain things aren't polite to discuss,* she says. I'm not sure which is the better approach.

It's funny, but I'm starting to feel *related* to Isabel already. It doesn't matter that my mom and aunt picked her out from a little lineup of babies. She's my cousin now and forever. I whisper in Isabel's ear that when I go to college in New York, I promise to take her everywhere, to the movies and the Central Park Zoo and Times Square. It's nice to feel at home with someone and know the bond can't be broken just because you have an argument. Maybe one day I'll get to tell Isabel about this early time together. I want to share with her the story of my life, the way Saul is doing with me.

Isabel's putting on weight and this makes Mom and Tía Paloma happy. I volunteer to change her diapers. It's hard to do with one hand (the other is pinching my nostrils) but Mom helps me out and Isabel acts excited to see me. Her skin is so soft. I've never felt anything as soft in my life. I lend her Lena, my stuffed cow, to help her sleep. Then we sing Isabel one of Mom's nonsense lullabies. Everyone's off-key but at least we're laughing again.

> I love you, a bushel and a peck,
> A bushel and a peck and a hug around the neck,
> I said I love you, a bushel and a peck,
> A bushel and a peck and a hug around the neck,
> I said I love you a bushel and a peck every day,
> Every day, every day day day day day.

After Isabel is tucked in and asleep, Mom starts getting nostalgic for when I was a baby. "You grew so chubby from nursing!" she reminisces. "And whenever you were on the verge of a growth spurt, you'd nurse eight hours a day. I really learned what it feels like to be a cow!"

I roll my eyes, but I still listen.

"You were so plump and adorable that people called you the Gerber Baby," Mom continues. "Only your evil stare unsettled them. People would try to chuck you under the chin or pinch your cheek or make silly faces to try to get you to smile, but your expression wouldn't change. You'd narrow your eyes and stare back at them, as if to say: 'Show me what else you can do.' Even Abuela was worried about it. She thought it might be a sign of a budding psychopath!"

Both of us laugh, though I've heard this a hundred times before. There's something nice about hearing stories of when I was a baby. It makes me feel like I have a history, like I belong somewhere. I've always felt pretty connected to my dad and his parents, especially Saul. But I guess I do have a Cuban side after all.

There's Internet service on the top floor of the hotel, so I sneak away to touch base with my friends. It's strange how life can simply go on without you. Here I am in a whole other country and nobody's the least bit curious about it. They assume that what I really want to know about is them. And they're right, to an extent. Véronique writes that her foil ball has grown to twenty-three inches in diameter and that her brother will probably be institutionalized after New Year's. Her parents are fighting constantly. *Sometimes I wish they'd just get it over with.* "It" meaning getting a divorce. I don't have the heart to tell her it opens up a whole new set of problems.

Probably the biggest news is from Squid-boy:

SB: My whole body is covered with cuts and abrasions.
Me: OMG, what happened?

SB: Guess who's taken up surfing?

Me: Who?

SB: That would be me.

Me: What?!

SB: Ha-ha, yeah, but I suck.

Me: No way!

SB: We're talking BIG SPLASH!!!

Me: So do we get to surf?

SB: Duh . . . work with me here . . .

Me: Okay, you're on.

This is so awesome, I can't stand it. Finally, someone to surf with! I laugh to think of Quincy in his full Squid-boy outfit trying to catch waves off Bay Street. It's going to be so much fun. Then he tells me he tried to rehearse the orchestra on his own, but it was a complete disaster. The violin section melted down trying to play "Pinhead." Good thing we still have almost two months to go till the concert.

My friends think Quincy has a crush on me, but I'm not so sure. He talks to me like I'm just a friend, nothing too personal. Besides, I've known him since third grade. When the girls ask Squid-boy who he likes, he jokes, *Girls don't get interesting until they're in college.* He does make me laugh more than anyone I know, except maybe for my dad. I like the way Quincy finds new ways of describing the ordinary. Like when a couple is making out and eating pizza at the same time (pretty common at lunch), he calls it "inhaling the cheese." Squid-boy comes up with a million of these a day.

But I don't get that fluttery feeling around him that I get around Eli or some of the skater boys. I want to ask my mom about this, but she would make way too big a deal of it, then give me the third degree. Squid-boy's mother, it turns out, is a lot like mine. She doesn't let him talk on the phone much, or take a bus, or hang out at the mall, or watch television, or own toy weapons, or spend a lot of time on the Internet, or *any*thing. Quincy suspects that our mothers were separated at birth.

Ten minutes later I'm instant messaging with my dad.

Me: Hey, Dad! How r u?

Dad: Yummy! Good to hear from you. *Como esta usted?*

Me: Nice Spanish there, Dad.

Dad: How's your new cousin?

Me: She's soooo cute.

Dad: And the poop factor?

Me: Duh. She's human . . .

Dad: Guess what?

Me: ???

Dad: We got a gig at the Whisky A Go-Go this Saturday. Some band dropped out and they called us.

Me: That's great, Dad!

CRISTINA GARCÍA

Dad: Could be our big break.

Me: U gonna play "Shoebox"?

Dad: Yep. Wrote a couple of new songs, too.

Me: Titles?

Dad: One's called "Worst President Ever." The other: "Cambodian Souvenirs."

Me: Whoa, can't wait to hear them.

Dad: They're intense and

Me: Funny, right? How's Saul?

Dad: A little worse than yesterday, but he's hanging in there. He misses you. We all do.

Me: I miss you guys too.

Dad: Saul keeps trying to tell everyone the story of his life. He's a broken record about it.

Me: You sure he's okay?

Dad: Don't worry, he'll still be here when you get back. So . . . how's your mom?

Me: On a pork rind kick.

Dad: ????

Me: U better believe it!

It's true. The last couple of days all health food concerns are out the window and Mom's been chomping on pork rinds—*chicharrones* in Spanish. Have you ever seen pork rinds? Blistered pigskin attached to nothing. It's beyond disgusting. Mom's also eating fried plantains, refried beans, fried chicken, fried eggs, and *crema* over everything. Plus, she's obsessively working out at the gym. I think she's bulking up for a fight with one of those military guys. Or preparing for the inevitable hand-to-hand combat with an attacking shark off the California coast. She's also planning a trip to the mountains. Here, they call them the "highlands." I'd prefer to stay in the hotel with Tía Paloma and Isabel, but Mom is forcing me to go with her.

On Thursday morning we get on a bus for Lake Atitlán. When I told Mom earlier this morning that I was worried about Saul, she said, "You watch, he'll outlive us all." But I don't believe her. She likes him okay, but I don't think she respects him that much. It's probably because Saul has let Hiroko support him for all these years. It's a sore point with her. Mom makes a lot more money than my dad, and she doesn't respect men who don't pull their financial weight. I mean, what's my allowance? Eight dollars a week? Mom pays me religiously, but Dad, who's supposed to give me only two dollars a week, never pays me at all. He likes to joke that he's a deadbeat, but Mom doesn't find this the least bit funny.

The bus is rusty and jangly and crowded. We hit so many bumps that my butt hurts. It's probably bruising my brain, too.

"Ow, I can't afford to lose any more brain cells," I whine after a particularly bad pothole. "If I don't get good scores on the SATs, it'll be your fault."

Mom hates it when I complain. To her, the more miserable a journey, the more authentic it is. I say an air-conditioned bus with seat cushions is no less authentic. A taxi would be even better. But Mom likes to travel with the locals.

"This is the best way to get to know a country, Yumi," she says stiffly. "You get to see how *real* people live."

In El Salvador we crisscrossed the country on the back of a flatbed truck. In Vietnam we went from one end of a river valley to the other on top of an elephant (Mom still has neck problems from *that* joyride). In Bolivia she insisted on keeping pace with the market women and ended up with nosebleeds from the altitude.

Why should today be any different?

It's a four-hour ride into the mountains, diesel fumes spewing the whole way. Mom points out the parrots and mango trees and God-knows-what-else in the passing villages, but it's all I can do to keep breathing. What I do notice are the dogs—skin-and-bones scrawny, foraging in piles of garbage—and the vultures circling overhead. So this is the big cultural experience?

It's strangely quiet on the bus, in spite of all the people. When they do talk, I can't understand a word. These local dialects, Mom says, are variations of ancient Mayan. She tells me that my great-grandmother on her father's side of the family came from these highlands. "Her blood runs in our veins," she says, beaming. It's another one of her "one world" moments.

It's early afternoon by the time we get to Panajachel, a town on the shores of Lake Atitlán. Once you get past the hustling vendors—nearly impossible for my mom—it's actually a pretty place. There are volcanoes everywhere, and the water is this amazing shade of blue. Birds are chattering and screeching like there's a convention or something. I watch the gentle waves on the lake, and it makes me miss the ocean and surfing and the sting of salt in my eyes. I guess I'm pretty homesick.

We decide to have lunch at a lakefront restaurant.

Mom's order: fried fish, fried plantains, refried beans, yellow rice, two pork tamales, and some local drink made with hibiscus flowers.

My order: corn tortillas, plain white rice, an orange soda.

Mom wants to go out on a boat right after we eat. Storm clouds are gathering on the far side of the lake, but it's warm and sunny on our side so she decides to take a chance. A half hour of vigorous bargaining gets us a dilapidated motorboat christened *El Milagro*. Personally, I think it's going to take a miracle for the thing to float. But float it does, even after the captain—I use the term loosely—loads up the boat with a leashed pig and a couple of crates filled with chickens. Mom starts arguing with the guy, saying that these animals shouldn't be included in our fare, and he knocks a few *quetzals* off the price.

It's good to get out on the water after being cooped up on that bus. The air smells really clean, like right after it rains in Los Angeles, but the noise of the motor grinds out any other sound. Soon the diesel fumes interfere with my breathing, but I get used to it after a while and try to enjoy myself. Ribbons of smoke rise from the thatch-roofed huts on the shore. Fishing boats bob peacefully behind us, casting their nets. There are lots of pine trees on the mountainsides (I don't ever think of them as living in the tropics), and birds I've never seen before flit past our boat.

Straight ahead the water and sky are merging into an angry gray mass. Mom wants to go to Santiago Atitlán, where she's heard there are great paintings and tapestries for sale at the market. The village is tucked between two volcanoes, and I'm curious if they've ever erupted. Mom asks the captain, but he looks at her blankly. The wind picks up, and our boat struggles against it, still aimed at Santiago Atitlán. The pig wakes up suddenly and starts snorting and straining against its leash. This gets the chickens flustered, and puffs of reddish feathers float up and away in the wind. I look at Mom but she's stonily facing forward, as if to say: *Don't even think of turning around.*

I get a sinking feeling in my stomach. A few drops of rain hit my face, and then with no warning, it's raining harder than I've ever seen in my life. We're talking three hundred percent precipitation here, whipping and mean. The rumble of thunder is deafening, and lightning flashes on top of the volcanoes. It's like some crazy horror movie where the unsuspecting tourists anger the local gods. Mom looks like a deranged general at the helm of the boat—George Washington crossing the Potomac comes to mind—except she doesn't have a clue what she's doing. I'm soaked to the bones. My clothes feel as thin and soggy as paper.

The boat is shuddering, then it starts rocking violently as water collects on the bottom. The captain throws me a bucket, and I start bailing for all I'm worth. It's hard because the pig keeps getting in my way, trying to see if I'm hiding oats or something. I'm ready to throw him overboard. Is it my imagination, or are we sinking? The storm is coming at us, and I can't see much past my arms. Seaweed and foam fill my bucket, and I'm hopeful we're close to shore. Mom is silently moving her lips, but I can't make out the words. I imagine her apologizing to me: *I'm so sorry, cookie-pie. I just wanted us to have a little fun, see the world. I didn't expect it to kill us.* My rage against her makes me bail faster.

How can I die before saying good-bye to Saul? Nobody knows who we are here or how to contact my dad or my grandparents or Tía Paloma. If I die, it means I won't get to go to college in New York and hang out with Isabel when she can actually carry on a conversation. How could we just drown here, nameless, in the middle of this Guatemalan lake, our watery graves unmarked? Would our bodies wash up on shore? Are there piranhas here like in the Amazon that'll eat our flesh to the bone?

CRISTINA GARCÍA

Dad will get even more depressed. And Saul—who will he tell the rest of his life story to? We barely got through half of it, and there's still so much more to go—forty years' worth, in fact. Maybe there'll be an announcement in the newspaper or on the nightly news with our pictures. I imagine my friends hearing about the drowning: Squid-boy forlorn and surfing by himself in Venice; Véronique erecting a shrine in my honor; Kara and Eli finally getting together in shared grief over me.

How could Mom do this to me?

Hang in there, Yumi girl, hang in there. It's Saul's voice talking to me inside my head. How does he know where I am? Does this mean he's already dead? A big crash flings me back against the chicken crates. We've hit some sort of rock, and water is flooding the boat now. "Jump! Jump!" the captain screams at us in possibly the only word of English he knows. I look at my mother, and she looks back at me and nods. We both take the plunge; her first, then me.

The water is cold and churning but it tastes sweet, and I remember I'm in a lake, not the ocean. I get tossed and turned, and the breath is beaten from my body. I must be swallowing a gallon of water. Luckily, I'm used to this from surfing and wait until I come right side up. To my shock, my feet touch bottom. It's soft and sandy and welcoming. I look around for my mother and see her sputtering on the shore like a beached sea mammal, seaweed dangling from her shoulders, clutching her purse with all her might.

"Are you okay, sweetheart?" Mom asks, trying to stagger toward me but falling back on the sand.

I settle down next to her and put my head in her lap. Water is trickling out of my nose and mouth. The rain has let up a little, and we see the captain dragging the remains of his boat to shore. One chicken weirdly skitters across the surface of the lake and disappears into the underbrush. It seems that the pig and the other chickens didn't make it. The captain waves at us eagerly, probably still hoping to get paid.

"Mom?"

"Yes, darling?" She smooths my hair as best she can.

I look up at her face, streaked with mascara. "I want to go home. I want to see Saul."

∞∞

Hey, Yumi girl! It's good to see you, kid! Whoa, I missed you something awful. I feel better already just looking at you. You got taller down in Guatemala. What did they feed you down there? You grew so much on rice and beans? Heh-heh, that's hard to believe. And look at that mask! You got it for me? Well, thanks a lot, kid. Makes me feel like a tiger. Ah, tiger, jaguar, they're all big cats, as far as I'm concerned.

You know, nobody around here wants to hear my stories. Only you, little one, only you. The truth is, all this remembering is making me dizzy and I'm not half done with the telling. Yesterday I got weak in the knees helping myself to a little crumb cake. Collapsed right there on the kitchen floor. Couldn't stop coughing neither. Nearly gave Hiroko a stroke. You know her blood pressure is sky-high with all the stress.

Me and Hiroko's wedding? It wasn't no big deal. Her family came to the justice of the peace with us. Dinner afterward at the best steak house in Yokohama. Your grandmother looked stunning. Took my breath away, she did. At the last minute she decided to go for broke and wear a traditional Japanese wedding costume. I hardly recognized her. She looked like one of them geisha girls. For our honeymoon we went up to the hot springs in Nikko. Fancy place. Ten servants for every guest. Pampered up the wazoo.

Our first months together were pretty good. I moved us into a bigger suite at my hotel. Hiroko loved it. She called room service every five minutes just to see someone come to the door with a silver tray. She ordered everything on the menu, starting with the appetizers and ending with the apple pie. Hiroko put on a few pounds, but it only made her more beautiful. She doted on me, too, insisted on shaving me herself. Yeah, she shaved me better than any barber ever did. But it didn't last long. Nothing ever does, kid. There ain't no guarantees. Mostly, you have to work real hard to keep things right for yourself.

Anyway, Hiroko started feeling lonely sitting around the hotel all day long. She wanted us to have our own apartment, so I get us an apartment, a high-class one on the boulevard near the consulates and whatnot. She wanted to fix up the apartment, so we fixed up the apartment, sparing no expense. Chandeliers, silk curtains, French furniture—you name it. Your grandmother might've been selling soup on the streets, but she still had fine taste. Only the best for her, I said. If truth be told, you could buy things for a song then, but it was still plenty of dough for the times.

After the apartment was finished, Hiroko wanted to work again, but I said no way. I didn't want her hustling soup up and down the streets of Yokohama. Then she tells me she wants to work as a shopgirl selling gloves or jewelry, but I put my foot down. I was an old-fashioned guy and didn't want my wife working. Well, Hiroko didn't like it one bit. That's when I got the first of her silent treatments. Much worse than an argument. Much worse than a firing squad, if you ask me.

I don't understand women, Yumi. What I appreciate is a straight shooter. I don't know if it's the hormones or what, but . . . You calling me a sexist, little one? Heh-heh. I guess your mother taught you good. Yeah, you're defending yourself all right. Look, Yumi girl, it's a generational thing. I read the paper, I try to keep up with the times. But the old ways still live inside me fighting with the new ways, you know what I'm saying? Wait until you have your own grandkids and they start calling you old-fashioned. Grandma Yumi, heh-heh. I want to be around to see that.

Me and Hiroko had us some good times, though. Your grandmother was what they call a "party girl" today. You laugh, but it's true. She got a taste for the high life and took to it like a fish to water. If it were up to her, Hiroko would've gone to a different nightclub every night. You gotta remember she was barely twenty-one and hadn't seen nothing of the world. We used to go hear the American big bands

CRISTINA GARCÍA

play in Tokyo. They were just getting popular in Japan. That's when we saw Benny Goodman. People went crazy for Yankee anything. If you can't beat 'em, join 'em—that was the thinking. Hiroko could do a pretty mean jitterbug.

We got season tickets to the baseball games in Yokohama, and Hiroko didn't miss a single one. Her throat got raw from shouting for her favorite players. Extreme fan, your grandmother. Horse racing was starting to take off in Japan too, and I bought myself a couple of thoroughbreds. Never turned them into champions, but they didn't do too badly, neither. Let's just say they kept themselves in oats and hay. Sometimes I wonder how me and Hiroko's world got so small when it started out so big.

But change is inevitable, kid. No use trying to run from it or pretending to keep everything the same. It's a law of nature. Things die if they stand still too long. They get stagnant, like an old pond. That don't mean that everything will get better right away. But everything happens for a reason. In the long run, it usually turns out for the best.

By the end of 1959, though, things weren't going too good for me, to tell the truth. And what's the point of telling you anything if it ain't the truth, right? The Japanese government knew I was wheeling and dealing, but they didn't make a stink about it until then. It was the mayor of Yokohama who made my life miserable. Yuto Ezure was his name. Little rabbity guy, was sweet on Hiroko. He decided it was time to pick on me: the ganji, the foreigner.

It came down to this: The Japanese government told me I needed to pack my bags and leave the country. The last thing I wanted to do was leave. Yokohama had become more of a home to me than even Brooklyn. But we packed our bags, shipped our furniture to a warehouse in California, cleaned out my bank accounts, and headed for the airport. When we were settled in the plane and taxiing down the runway, your grandmother leaned against me and said, "We're going to have a baby."

WE'VE MOVED, AND IT'S HORRIBLE. MOM RENTED THIS REALLY depressing two-bedroom apartment in Pacific Palisades with gross wall-to-wall carpet and old-people clutter and kitchen appliances from the last century. There was even a portable toilet right in the middle of the master bedroom. Mom and I kept pushing it back and forth into each other's rooms, laughing and joking, but in the end, she hid it in a closet. She says that a famous philosopher lived here and died in the very bed she's sleeping in! His widow, who's on the East Coast now, is a small-time literary agent. In any case, Mom assures me, the apartment is filled with great books—of course, nothing I want to read.

My bed is hard, and there isn't enough light, and I can't practice my clarinet after eight o'clock because it disturbs the retirees in the building. I don't understand how we went from living in a beautiful ocean-view home to this dump.

"Why do we have to live here?" I whine on our second night there.

"Because it's all I can afford right now," Mom says simply.

"How long do we have to stay?"

"I told you already—until you graduate."

"And then?"

"*Mi amor*, I don't know yet. I'm still waiting to hear about that teaching job."

"We're not moving to Texas, are we? Because I swear I'll go live with Dad!" I'm on the verge of tears again, but I try to hold them back.

"No, we're not moving to Texas. Eventually, Jim will move to California with us."

"Dad thinks you're just tired of living in L.A., that you could stay if you wanted."

"Your father—," Mom starts angrily, but she thinks better of it and softens her tone. "Your dad loves you very much. Nothing in the world will ever change that, no matter where we end up."

Not only are we living in a new place, but everything feels different to me since we got back from Guatemala. I've been having this strange dream every night about an owl talking to me from the top of a tree. It talks and talks, but I can only make out about every tenth word. "Brown" comes up a lot; so does "fire." I strain to hear more, but other forest sounds interfere. I wonder if it has anything to do with our near drowning on Lake Atitlán. I've heard Mom retell the story a thousand times, each time more outrageously. It's so embarrassing, especially when she looks to me to back her up. *Isn't that right, Yumi? Isn't that the way it happened?*

In her latest version she referred to our accident as a "shipwreck." The captain was straight out of *Moby-Dick*, and she's now claiming that the chickens broke out of their crates and flew to shore like a flock of seagulls. Do I need to mention that Mom's a big fan of magical realism?

Tía Paloma is still stuck in bureaucratic limbo in Guatemala trying to bring Isabel home. It's going on a month now, but my aunt is determined not to leave the country without her baby. Tía Paloma reminds me a lot of my mom in this way. When either of them wants something, they stop at nothing to get it. I miss Isabel. I never realized how nice it would be to have a cousin. I used to pester my mother about wanting a sister or brother—actually, an older brother would've been perfect—but she would just smile at me sadly and tell me it wasn't possible anymore.

Even when I see friends fighting with their siblings, I think that at least they have someone to fight with. If I had a brother or sister, there'd be at least one other kid on the planet who was just like me. Even the director of that Hapa Project said he'd never met someone who was part Cuban, part Japanese, part Russian Jew. I wonder how Isabel will figure out who she is and where she belongs. A tiny, brown-skinned kid from Guatemala trying to make herself heard among all those hyper, fast-talking New Yorkers. I wish I could be around to help her feel at home, to not feel so alone.

It's a relief to go to my dad's place after the claustrophobia of the apartment. His loft is in this semiconverted piano warehouse. He got it from a client in exchange for tuning his pianos every month. The ceilings are thirty feet high, and the broken windows are patched with cardboard. Sometimes it feels creepy after dark, like the night is trying to push its way in. But mostly, it's a cool space, great for playing rock-'n'-roll. Dad isn't much on ceremony. The only things he really cares about are music, movies, and books. There's plenty of all three here to keep me busy.

My father decides to give me one of his occasional bass lessons. Playing electric bass seems simple to me after playing clarinet. There isn't even any music to read. Dad never learned. He figures out every song by ear. The notes aren't hard to memorize, but the attitude you can't fake. That's the big difference between punk bands that made an impact— the Ramones, the Sex Pistols, the Dead Kennedys, to name just a few—and the countless ones who didn't, who just went through the motions. *It's hard to explain, but you know it when you hear it.* That's what Dad says. He's adamant on this point.

At the end of the lesson we both try playing "I Wanna Be Your Shoebox" full out—Dad's on guitar, I'm on bass—and it's a blast. Only, Millie scuttles off and hides under my bed.

Tonight his band, Armageddon, is coming over to rehearse. Dad's tired from an emergency tuning of a Steinway grand at some Catholic college near the airport. He said this psycho nun screamed at him the whole time he was working. But his band badly needs to rehearse. They've got another gig at the Whisky A Go-Go this weekend and a battle of the bands at the Knitting Factory later this month. It's amazing how Armageddon keeps plugging away. Dad's been in the band for years—and they've come close to getting recording deals a few times. But something always goes wrong.

Last year they finally got so fed up with the rejection that they cut their own CD. Mom bought a dozen and gave them out as stocking stuffers to her friends. She joked that nobody ever thanked her for the Christmas gifts. The big problem isn't the band—which is fast and tight—it's the lead singer. He's a disaster—an unsightly, sweating, leering mess (Mom's description) in a three-piece sharkskin suit. He can't sing, either but he funds the band.

Everyone drifts in around nine. I get high fives and my hair tousled a lot. *How's it going, Yumi?* I've become a sort of mascot for the band, although it's not like I've brought them good luck or anything. Ruby, the backup singer, has taken me under her wing and offers me fashion and makeup tips.

Her voice is low and growly but has some swing to it. Once in seventh grade Ruby lent me one of her trashy outfits, and I went to school that way. Mom had to pick me up at the principal's office a half hour after I arrived at school. It was one of my parents' worst fights.

The band starts off with a couple of my dad's new songs. They've transformed "I Wanna Be Your Shoebox" into an even faster, more aggressive song than it was before. Since I helped with the lyrics, Danny, the lead singer, promised me a song-writing credit whenever their album comes out. Recently, Dad wrote another song called "A Fine Desolation," about a guy who takes to drinking too many carbonated beverages and showing poodles after his wife leaves him. Humiliation and unrequited love—those are my dad's main themes. The band plays "A Fine Desolation" in a turbocharged country-punk style.

WHEN YOU LEFT ME THERE WAS NO PLACE ELSE FOR
ME TO GO
BUT THE DOGS, THEY WERE WANTING BEST OF SHOW
HOW COULD I SAY NO?
HOW COULD I SAY NO?

IT'S A FINE DESOLATION YOU LEFT ME IN
DOG HAIR EVERYWHERE AND A LITTER OF DRINKS
IT'S A FINE DESOLATION YOU LEFT ME IN
THE WAY I'M LIVIN' IS A SHAMEFUL SIN

"Hey, man, can't you lighten up those lyrics? This song is depressing," Fred the rhythm guitarist complains.

"Well, my life is exceedingly depressing, except for Yumi here," Dad shoots back. "I've got no other narrative." He told me once that there are a million ways to sing about love but, if you're lucky, just one way to live it.

"I'm tired of the same old same old." Fred backs off a little. He lights a cigarette, and the smoke blossoms in the air above him.

"If it makes a good song, then it's worth living through," Danny insists. "What else are we doing this for? Man, it's what makes you feel alive!" He juts his fist in the air.

I think Danny would be a lot more convincing if he weren't constantly hogging the limelight. I mean, he has to be the center of attention every waking moment. The guy practically *swallows* the microphone when he sings.

"So whaddya wanna do, Fred? Sing 'Girls Just Want to Have Fun'?" This is Ruby chiming in, adjusting her lipstick in a compact mirror. "Of course it's depressing. Have you looked at the world lately?"

"Nah, Austin's just annoyed because none of the radio stations have picked up 'Shoebox,'" Fred says sarcastically. "How many rejections you rack up, Austin—twenty, fifty, a hundred?"

"Why don't you just shut up, huh?" Dad is glaring at Fred, and I think he might cry, but he doesn't. "You're no better than my old man."

I feel bad hearing my dad talk about Saul this way. Saul means well and he wants my dad to be happy, but neither of them is exactly the most diplomatic person in the world. Dad doesn't think Saul cares about him. But it's not true. Why did Saul stay home with him all those years if he didn't care? Sometimes I think they're both way too stubborn to get along.

Later I retreat to the other end of the warehouse to finish my homework. I'm having a hard time concentrating, so I instead stare out the windows at the night sky. It's a big load of dark, as my dad would say. You never see a lot of stars in L.A.—it's too polluted for that—but I like to imagine them there anyway. It's weird to think that the few stars I do see may not even exist anymore. I mean, they're light-years away, and by the time I see them, they might already be burned out. The moon is another story, though. Fat and waxy and yellow-looking, almost full. It's a stage hog too. If Danny could be a celestial body, he would definitely be the moon.

There's a liquor store on the corner, and its neon sign blinks red all night long. I can hear it buzzing from my bed. Some guy comes out of the store and starts laughing so hard, I think he'll empty himself out. He drives off in a gold-trimmed Cadillac. The parking lot is vacant now. On the other side of it is the Happy Triplets Motel. Sometimes when I can't sleep, I watch people going in and out of there for hours. Dad is up until five in the morning, so I feel pretty safe spying.

Dad always naps before taking me to school, then sleeps until noon. Tonight I'm tired and conk out around eleven. I want to get up early because I'm meeting Squid-boy for our first surf lesson on Bay Street. My dad's place is only four blocks from the beach—close enough to smell the salt air and, after a rainstorm, to smell the sewage washing out to sea. I've been keeping my fingers crossed that it wouldn't rain before tomorrow. And it hasn't—yes! Sweet dreams, sweet dreams, sweet dreams!

The morning is cold and overcast as I ride my bike to the beach, balancing my surfboard under my left arm. It's five thirty, but I'm wide awake. Venice is quiet except for a few homeless people stirring through the garbage dumps to see what the restaurants threw out last night. Squid-boy is waiting for me on the boardwalk, all suited up and ready to go. He looks like a giant seal, complete with a waterproof wristwatch. He grins at me, and I grin right back at him. Every last cent of his birthday money went to buy his used Anderson longboard, which is very cool. It feels funny being with just him. We're usually with the orchestra or in a group of friends. It makes me nervous, but excited nervous, not scared nervous.

"Okay, let's catch some waves!" he shouts, and sprints down the beach, upsetting some sleeping seagulls. Suddenly, they're squawking and circling over him. It's like a scene right out of an Alfred Hitchcock movie. What if the birds attack and peck him to death our first day out?

"Run!" I scream, and chase him into the ocean. The waves are good—small but kind of crumbly. I don't think I'll embarrass myself too badly. It's true that I've been talking up surfing like I'm some big expert. It's easy to do when nobody else is around to keep you honest. I admit I've exaggerated a little. It's something I inherited from my mother.

Quincy and I dive in at the same time and start paddling toward the first break. There's a lot of seaweed clumping up the whitewash, and it's hard to get through the gunk. By the time we're out far enough, we look like creatures from the Black Lagoon.

"So, bog girl, what do we do now?" Squid-boy is grinning at me again, grinning so hard, it looks like his face might split in two.

"Follow me," I laugh, and maneuver the board so I'm facing the shore. I explain the whole sit-and-spin thing, how you need to keep an eye on the waves behind you but stay in position to swim fast enough to catch them. "When a good swell comes along, paddle like mad and jump up on your board."

We don't have to wait too long for a nice set of waves. Squid-boy is a strong paddler, but his balance is off and he falls backward every time. I tell him to center his weight and scoot forward, but nothing seems to help. He can't get up no matter what he does.

CRISTINA GARCÍA

"Let me just watch you for a while," he says with a smile.

Okay, the show is on. My reputation is at stake here. I imagine I'm on the North Shore of Oahu for the Women's World Championship, lined up right next to Layne Beachley and Keala Kennelly. I suck it up big-time and just do it. Wave after wave comes up under me like magic, and I ride them crosswise to shore like I was born doing this. I try not to think too hard. When something good happens, Mom says, just enjoy it. It's a gift from the universe.

"Yahoo! Ride 'em, girl!" Squid-boy shouts, and I can tell he's really pleased for me, not competitive like boys get or jealous like girls can get. He's as excited for me as I am for myself. I wish we could've gotten this on film. Nobody would believe it. Hey, I don't believe it!

The ocean calms down for a while, and I paddle over to Squid-boy. He's sitting up on his board and claps like I've just given a brilliant concert. He tries to make it a standing ovation but tips over into the sea and comes up sputtering.

"You're amazing," Quincy says in a quieter voice.

"You bring me good luck," I say. "I've never surfed so well in my life."

"Liar."

"I swear to God!"

"You know what this means then?" He narrows his eyes at me.

"What?"

"I've got to surf with you every day, surfer queen."

"Surfer queen—I like the sound of that," I laugh.

We start paddling toward shore. Most of the seaweed has drifted away, and we trudge through the whitewash dragging our boards. When we get to the beach, Quincy collapses on his back and stares straight up at the morning sky. The clouds look like wisps of cotton candy against the deepening blue. I lie down too, not too close, but close enough to hear what he says next. The sand is wet and scratchy against the back of my head, and my feet itch something awful.

I try to bring up the orchestra, but Quincy puts a finger to his lips. "I don't like to mix business with pleasure," he jokes. Then he gets serious all of a sudden. "Yumi, I was just wondering . . ."

"Mmmm . . ."

"Would you like to go to the dance with me on Friday?" He blurts this out quickly, and the words melt together, sounding like: Wouldyouliketogotothedancewithmeonfriday? Then he takes a deep breath. "I mean, we don't have to freak dance or anything."

I hesitate, dismissing the picture of Eli that pops into my head. The lyrics to "I Wanna Be Your Shoebox" flood my brain, and I can't think straight. This is the big dance he's talking about, the Winter Madness Ball. Then to my surprise—and to Quincy's—I say, "Sure."

◾

CRISTINA GARCÍA

At school I go around all morning like I have this big secret. I don't know why I haven't told anyone yet about going to the Winter Madness Ball with Squid-boy. I guess I want to keep the news to myself a little longer, make it last before it's up for public consumption. It's Wednesday at lunchtime, and the yard is abuzz with gossip. The number two topic of the day for my friends is the latest calamity to strike the orchestra. Most of the violinists, led by Sonya Gutierrez, have defected to form their own strings ensemble. They've charged that we've sold out to the pressures of pop culture and that we should stick to classical music. To make matters worse, they're lobbying all the other string players to follow suit. Fortunately, the cellos and double basses aren't budging, but the violas, typically, are on the fence. So how are we supposed to have an orchestra without violins? Quincy and I have got a ton of work to do today to convince them to stay.

Our concert is still on for Valentine's Day, and our ticket committee has put in an order for five hundred tickets. We've got rehearsals scheduled every single weekend between now and then. How could the violinists do this to us? It isn't fair!

The number *one* topic at school today has nothing to do with the orchestra at all. It's about the Winter Madness Ball: who's going with whom, who got rejected, who's wearing what, and whose parents will be chaperoning. Everyone groans when we find out that Eli's mother, the parole officer, is head chaperone. She'll probably show up with handcuffs and a nightstick. Today is definitely the last respectable day to ask anyone to the dance. After this any overture and/or acceptance will have the whiff of desperation, something to avoid at all costs.

Kara has practically draped herself over Eli near the twiggy rosebushes, hoping for an invite. So far, nothing. A lot of the boys are saying they're going "stag," thinking that sounds cool. I think they're just nervous making a statement about who they like. Squid-boy is on the longest line in the Western Hemisphere for chips and guacamole. I noticed him sneaking glances at me in math class. It's like suddenly we've both become super shy around each other.

Eli disentangles himself from the tentacled Kara and comes over to where I'm standing with a bag of Gummi worms. The alert signal goes out, and Kara glares at me from the rosebushes.

"Hey," he says. "Want some?"

"Got any orange ones?"

This is an old joke between us. He *never* has any orange ones.

"Nah." He smiles.

"Well, okay." I act like I'm doing him this big favor.

"So . . . did your mom get that job yet?" he asks me.

"That was random." I start laughing, chewing on a worm.

"Not as random as you might think."

"No?"

"You see, your mother is messing up my long-term plans."

"Tell me about it."

"No, I'm serious. I was, uh, planning on asking you to the senior prom."

"You mean the one four years from now?" I try to keep a straight face.

"That very one." He holds up a finger like he's trying to figure out which way the wind is blowing. "But since I'm not sure you'll be around then . . . I thought . . . uh . . . I thought . . . maybe . . ."

Oh no, this isn't happening!

"I thought . . . uh . . . that maybe you could go with me to the dance *this* week?"

His voice squeaks adorably, and he looks down at the ground and drops the rest of the Gummi worms all over his sneakers. Panic overtakes me. *Think, think fast! Don't accept, but don't discourage him.* I wish that I had the movie camera to play this back again. Or that I could stop time so I can figure out what to do. Everything's happening way too fast. At that exact moment Kara comes right up to us, followed by Squid-boy with a double order of chips and guacamole to share.

"So wassup, dogs?" Squid-boy says in the worst rapper voice ever.

"Well, I was just asking Ms. Yumi here to the dance."

Kara bursts into tears and runs over to tell our friends.

Squid-boy stops in mid-chew, his half-eaten mouthful of

chips visible to all. "But she already said she's coming with me. Tell him, Yumi."

Eli looks at him, then turns to me with question mark eyes. My face gets hot and I open my mouth, but nothing comes out. Eli's surprise rinses away quickly, and he shrugs like it's no big deal. Meanwhile, Squid-boy's smile turns to disbelief. He glares at me for so long that I feel as if he's burning a hole in my forehead. Then he stomps off without saying another word. I don't know what to do. I'm tongue-tied and miserable, and everyone is mad at me. I try to come up with a good explanation for what just happened. But I can't. I don't even understand it myself.

You sure you want me to go on? I don't know, Yumi. It ain't easy reliving the hard times, and that's what came up for me and your grandmother. Hardest times I ever knew except for the year my mother died. Harder than the Depression, harder than the war because I only had myself to fend for then. Look at it this way: I was nearly fifty years old with a wife and a kid on the way. And it was sayonara *to the good life in Japan. Yeah, those days were gone forever.*

First place we settled was New York. I wanted to show Hiroko around my old stomping grounds. We stayed at the St. George Hotel in Brooklyn Heights, not too far from where your mother grew up. It was a nice residential hotel then, before it went over to welfare cases. There was a barber on the ground floor who

CRISTINA GARCÍA

was top-drawer—not as good as Hiroko, mind you, but he gave a decent shave.

Hiroko was so impressed with him that she asked him to do her face. No, she wasn't no bearded lady or nothing. Some Japanese women just like getting rid of their peach fuzz for a smoother complexion. Well, when Hiroko sat down in that barber's chair, the whole neighborhood came to watch. She was so embarrassed that she ran out the back with the shaving cream on her face. Still makes me laugh to think about it. After that she learned to shave herself with a straight razor.

I wasn't too worried about money for a couple of months. We took in the sights, saw a few shows, and I looked up my old cronies from before the war. Most of them had moved away or died. Your grandmother loved the Brooklyn Botanic Garden, and she took walks there almost every day. She liked the rose garden best. Sometimes she'd sit there rubbing her stomach and make a wish for our baby. Hiroko ate a lot of fish too, because she said it was good brain food. And it's true—your dad turned out pretty smart.

But everything in New York cost five, ten, twenty times more than it did in Japan, and my money was disappearing fast. Today things are just the opposite. A cup of coffee costs ten bucks in Tokyo. Imagine that! On top of my money running low, I felt like a nobody back home. I wasn't used to that no more. I'd been a somebody in Yokohama, a somebody you needed to know to get things done. People there respected me. In New York nobody gave me the time of day.

We went to stay with my brother in Ithaca for a while. Remember, Frank was a chemistry professor at Cornell—good school, that Cornell. But he couldn't help me. His wife, Selma, took an instant dislike to us. Selma made our lives miserable. Kept dropping hints about us leaving until we couldn't take it no more. We got outta there fast.

I don't know what possessed me, but I decided to take Hiroko back to the West Coast. Figured I'd start out fresh. But I couldn't get a job nowhere. I'm talking a real job, running a business or on the docks at San Pedro. You gotta believe me when I tell you I pounded the pavement. Meanwhile, Hiroko's belly was getting bigger and bigger. There were times I woke up in the middle of the night sweating up a storm. A pregnant wife. No job. The money trickling away like one of them egg timers. People kept asking me for my résumé, where I'd gone to college. Nobody'd ever asked me that in Japan. Could you get the job done? That was all that mattered.

The only work I got offered in Los Angeles was pumping gas. Me—pumping gas! It was unthinkable. When I look back, I realize I should've done whatever I had to do to keep us fed. Instead, I started going to the racetrack and the poker tables down in Gardena. But I'd lost my touch. Little by little, we sold off our stuff—Hiroko's jewelry, the tailored suits from Hong Kong, the French furniture we'd shipped over—until there was nothing left. It was tough on us. Hiroko cried every night.

I gotta hand it to your grandmother, though. She could've said a lot of things to me, things like: "So this is who you really are in

Checkout Receipt

National City Public Library
Circulation Department
For Renewals: (619)470-5821

02/24/15 05:20PM

****
Library Hours:
Mon- Thur 10am - 8pm
Sat - Sun 1pm - 5pm
Have a wonderful day
****

ITEM: 33835007405418
I wanna be your shoebox /
Due Date: 03/24/15
YA
GARCIA

TAL: 1

Date due information --- PLEASE KEEP

Library materials MUST be returned
to their home Library

your own country? A big shot in Japan; a nobody here. Washed up. A loser." But she never said nothing like that. And I was feeling it. Worse than you can imagine. But hard times were nothing new to Hiroko. She'd lived through World War II. Can't get much tougher than that. Let's just say your grandmother was a real class act, Yumi girl. She still is.

So where was I? Okay, me and your grandmother ended up in a motel room in Hawthorne that rented by the week. It wasn't no resort town, believe me. We were living ten miles from the beach, but it might as well have been a hundred. I wasn't in no mood to go parading down the boardwalk, if you know what I mean. There was a patch of crabgrass and dandelions in back of the motel, no bigger than one of my silk handkerchiefs. Hiroko asked the manager if she could take care of it, and he shrugged okay. In a month she had it blooming with flowers. Not just any flowers— orchids! The old girl's got a green thumb. You ever try those pears out back? I'm not much for fruit, little one, but your grandmother's pears are the best in the world. If she had a whole grove of them, we'd be living on easy street.

It was the middle of the night when Hiroko's water broke. There wasn't a soul in the world we could call except a taxi to take us to the hospital. I didn't have no insurance, no nothing, but they took us through the emergency room. I ain't gonna lie to you. It wasn't no fairy tale. We left that same morning with your dad bundled up in a baby blanket and a pom-pom hat the nurses gave us. No fanfare, no nothing, just another howling kid in the world.

I'd wanted a girl for selfish reasons. I didn't think I could teach a boy much about becoming a man. I didn't feel much like a man myself then.

Me and Hiroko had talked about different names—Jewish and Japanese ones, even Irish ones—but in the end, your dad was named by accident. When we got back to the motel, I flipped on the TV. There was a news report on about some tornado hitting Austin, Texas. "That's it!" Hiroko said, as happy as I'd seen her in months. "We name him Austin. Big tornado boy." What could I do? So I agreed, even though I thought it made him sound like a cowboy.

Four days later your grandmother left the motel room to look for work. She tied a sash around her belly to hold it in and told me to watch Austin. When I protested, she put a finger to her lips. "My turn now, Daddy," she said. She didn't care what I said no more. Something inside me died watching her go off like that.

My first day with Austin was a doozy, let me tell you. I'd never even held no baby before, much less took care of one. What if I killed him by mistake? Well, kid, it was me and the milk bottle and that colicky son of a gun all day long. Gave me a run for my money too. Kept pawing at my shirt. Didn't want no half-warmed formula from me. He cried and cried for all he was worth. It just about broke my heart.

I finally got him to sleep by letting him lie on my chest, just the two of us on the motel bed. I think it was my heartbeat that calmed

CRISTINA GARCÍA

him down. And I fell asleep right along with him. The sound of a key in the door woke us up. It was Hiroko. She'd managed to get a job on the assembly line of an electronics factory. Next day, Hiroko said, she would start at seven o'clock sharp.

A WEEK BEFORE VALENTINE'S DAY THE PRINCIPAL CALLS Quincy and me into his office before first period.

"I have bad news for you two," he says, shuffling papers around on his desk. "I got an offer from a movie studio to use our auditorium for a film they're making. They're going to pay us a lot of money. The bad news is that the shooting starts the morning of your concert."

"But you can't do that!" Quincy shouts, jumping out of his chair.

"We've been planning this for months, Mr. Minor," I say, trying to stay calm. "We've rehearsed a dozen times, sold tickets, printed programs, accepted advertisements, organized a bake sale—"

"Stopped a secession by the violinists!" Quincy interrupts.

"Told everyone!" I start losing it too.

"I know you're disappointed, but there's really nothing I can do. This will be a huge windfall for the school, and we need it badly."

"Are you kidding me?" Quincy is leaning over Mr. Minor's desk. "You gave us the okay months ago!"

"Now please sit down, Mr. Kaler. I'll be happy to write a letter of explanation to your advertisers."

"But you've ruined everything!" I say, barely audible.

Everything is going wrong. How could he do this to us? Quincy and Mr. Minor are arguing loudly when I get a sudden idea.

"Stop!" I shout. That gets their attention. "We need an alternate date."

"But the calendar is very congested. We—"

"Mr. Minor, if you don't find another concert date for us, the whole city will hear about this."

The principal is taken aback, but he reaches across his desk and starts flipping through a calendar. "Well, uh, the only open evening I have all spring is April first."

"April Fools' Day?" Quincy is beside himself. "Is this some kind of sick joke?"

"I'm very sorry, but this is all I can offer you right now."

"Wait." Now I'm standing too, though I only come up to Squid-boy's shoulders. "We'll take it."

"What?!" Quincy is indignant.

"We're not going to let anything or anybody stop our

CRISTINA GARCÍA

concert. If we have to postpone it, we will. It'll give us another month and a half to practice."

The principal is watching us. "Now there's a sensible girl—"

"You stay out of it," Quincy growls, and Mr. Minor shuts up.

"I'm serious, Squid. We can't just give up on this."

"But our name'll be mud. Nobody is going to believe anything we say anymore."

"Mr. Minor, you need to give this to us in writing," I say, all business.

"Of course, Yumi. Let me get my secretary to type it up right away."

"Your office will also pick up all the costs of duplicated materials for the new concert. You can take it out of the movie proceeds."

Mr. Minor starts to balk, but I look him straight in the eye, as if to say, *Your reputation is riding on this.*

"Well, okay, Yumi. That's reasonable enough."

"And, please, no more surprises. The orchestra is very important to us."

Outside the principal's office Quincy is looking at me like I've just conjured up the pope or something. "You were amazing!"

"Yeah, whatever." The amount of work we have to do now is overwhelming even to think about.

"No, I'm serious. You were awesome." Then Quincy backs off. This happens sometimes. He forgets he's supposed to be mad at me, and when he suddenly remembers, he cools off toward me again. It drives me crazy.

I stick my hand out to renew our pact of bringing back the orchestra. He takes it for a moment—his hand is cold and clammy—shakes it, and drops it just as quickly. But at least we're back on.

Things haven't been easy with Quincy since the Winter Madness disaster. It wasn't my fault that Eli asked me to the dance, but Quincy didn't want to talk about it. In the end, neither of us went. He couldn't avoid dealing with me altogether, though, because as co-chairs of the orchestra campaign, we had a concert to organize. But when he shows up on Venice Beach to surf, he makes a point of keeping his distance. Like last Saturday he was trying to surf down near the pier when his board jumped away from him, then flew back and knocked out one of his front teeth. He was bleeding everywhere and the lifeguard called for a stretcher, but Squid-boy acted like he didn't know me.

The rest of the day doesn't go much better. Predictably, once the news circulates, everyone in the orchestra is outraged and blaming Quincy and me for the last-minute cancellation. Half of them are saying they won't play the April Fools' Day concert; the other half aren't talking to me. It's going to take a lot of groveling to get everyone back on track. But what choice do I have? How can we let the orchestra disappear without a

CRISTINA GARCÍA

whimper? We need to make sure it's still around for the kids who come after us.

The weather is horrible enough to match my mood—overcast and sticky, practically tropical. Everyone's going around in shorts and tank tops, but it doesn't feel like spring yet. It's just humid and uncomfortable. The teachers are cranky and giving out too much homework, and everybody is arguing with one another. So what else can go wrong? At lunchtime I get a call from my dad telling me Saul isn't doing too well.

"He tried to take a bus to the racetrack but luckily Hiroko caught him in time," Dad says. "The excitement was too much for him."

Saul still thinks he's fifty. He refuses to use a cane, though he can hardly walk, and his appetite is nonexistent. All he can get down lately is some crumb cake and a mug of weak coffee in the morning. I'm going to call him tonight and tell him that maybe we can go to the track together one of these weekends. That should cheer him up. I tell Dad about the concert almost being cancelled, and he gets really angry. When I call and tell Mom, she's sympathetic and proud of how I handled things.

The only good news in the last twenty-four hours is that Tía Paloma finally got permission to bring Isabel home. Mom says we'll go visit them in New York next month. Last night Tía Paloma told Mom that Isabel has practically doubled in size. She's eating—and pooping!—up a storm and cooing like a little dove. I heard her myself on the telephone. I can't wait to see Isabel again. I miss her sour-milk scent and the way she waved her arms when I played her the clarinet. In her eyes I can do no wrong.

I keep thinking how strange it is that she'll grow up in Brooklyn, far away from the tropics. But Mom and Tía Paloma are convinced that Isabel was meant to be with us, to be my cousin, that *this* is her destiny. I wonder what that means, really. How do you balance what happens to you against what you make happen? Are they both a kind of destiny? I think about what Saul's been telling me. That life is not just about the hand you're dealt, but what you do with it.

After school on Valentine's Day, Mom and Jim are waiting for me with a huge bunch of balloons that say things like I LOVE YOU and BE MY SWEETHEART! I want to pretend I don't know them. But Mom is excited and pleased with herself and shouting, "Surprise!"—utterly oblivious to how ridiculous I look getting Valentine's Day balloons from my own mother in front of the whole school. I push the balloons out of the way and slide down the backseat as far as I can.

"Could you please turn on 103.1?"

"Sure, cookie-pie," Mom says.

The radio station is replaying *Jonesy's Jukebox* Valentine's Day special from earlier today. It turns out that Jonesy, who's incredibly sentimental for being an ex–Sex Pistol if you ask

CRISTINA GARCÍA

me, is playing nothing but sappy love songs. Is there no escape from this miserable holiday?

<u>Valentine's Day Tally for Yumi Ruíz-Hirsch:</u>
Cards: 0
Chocolates: 0
Notes from Secret Admirers: 0
Teddy Bears: 0
Anything with a Heart on It: 0

"Whose turn is it to choose a dinner place?" Mom chirps.

"Mine," I say.

"What's it going to be?"

The last thing I want to do is hang out with the two of them. But I'm in a perverse mood. Mom told me that Jim is originally from the Midwest and very particular about what he eats. As far as he's concerned, a baked potato is haute cuisine. Okay, I can't stand it anymore. I need to salvage a little fun from this dismal day.

"Sushi!" I announce.

"Sushi?" Mom and Jim chorus from the front seat. Do I imagine a gurgling sound coming from the back of Jim's throat?

An hour later we're at Nagao on San Vicente Boulevard. It's a neighborhood place and not very intimidating as far as sushi places go. In fact, the chefs here sound like they're from the Valley. *What can I get for you, dude?*

It's not nearly as much fun as I'd hoped because Mom orders everything cooked to protect Jim, to break him in easy: broiled eel and white rice, miso soup, California rolls—all the safe stuff. I want to see him slurping down quail eggs and salmon roe and yellowtail and raw tuna.

The sushi gets us to talking about surfing again.

"I hear the sharks are swimming closer to shore these days," Mom says. "I saw one myself on Yumi's last day of surf camp."

"Mom!" I start to whine. "You know it was a dolphin."

"They're armed and dangerous," she insists. "Have you seen their teeth?"

"I read about how one surfer in Australia got away from a great white by punching it in the nose," Jim chimes in, making a fist.

"Darling, it's not a boxing match!" Mom laughs.

Ugh! The one moment of comic relief for me comes when Jim tries to suck a bean out of an *edamame* pod and the whole thing goes flying and gets stuck on the front window.

But, of course, it can't stay light.

"*Mi amor*, I know you'll be disappointed to hear this, but I didn't get that teaching job here in L.A. I was terribly disappointed myself."

"What?!" I'm ready to burst into tears.

"I feel very bad about it, *gordita*, but I did everything I could. They told me they wanted someone with a Ph.D."

This can't be happening. I feel like my life's turning into a nightmare. There's no way I'm moving to Napa. I can't imagine going through high school without seeing my dad every day—or most days, anyway. Who's going to finish teaching me how to play electric bass? Or explain to me the fine points of one brand of instant ramen over another? Who's going to tell me stupid jokes? Or go skateboarding with me down the Venice boardwalk? Or tell me the history of every punk band that ever lived? Or watch the eleven o'clock news and tell me what's going on in the world? And that's just the tip of the iceberg.

"I'm not going," I mutter, but Mom doesn't hear me. She's chattering on like my whole world isn't collapsing into rubble.

"So you see, Yumi, it's our warmth and our presence that make a home. And we'll make another home in Napa. And Jim will be a part of that home."

"Why is *he* even here?" I practically shout, and that stops her.

Jim looks down at his uneaten rice. He wrings his hands together and looks like he's about to say something conciliatory, which only makes me angrier.

"Jim is going to help me drive a truck with our things to Napa this weekend."

For a long moment nobody says anything. I want to scream at them: *Nobody gets to touch my stuff!*

"We have more news, Yumi," Mom says quietly.

I look at her glumly. Will this dinner never end?

"We've set a date."

"A date?" I feel my chest tightening up.

"*Sí, mi amor*, Jim and I have set a date to get married. This June twenty-fourth."

Their eyes bore into mine, looking hopeful. What am I supposed to do? Stand up and cheer? Aren't things horrible enough without them expecting me to be happy for them? It's the worst, longest moment of my life.

"So," Jim says, all chipper, "I was still hoping you could teach me how to surf."

I have to suppress the urge to throw my pot of hot tea in his face. My life is over and he wants to go surfing with me? What is he, nuts?

And if he's trying to act like a dad, like *my* dad, he can forget about it. The fact is, I don't want Jim and my mom getting married, period. If I could be totally honest, I would tell him to scram—and a lot worse than that! Instead, I force a smile and ask to be excused. At first I just want to go to the bathroom and cry, but there's a line and I don't want to wait.

Without thinking twice, I sneak out the back door. I'm not sure where I'm going, only that I have to get away. I check my pockets for money. Three dollars and change. I'm on Twenty-sixth Street facing San Vicente Boulevard when I see a Big Blue Santa Monica bus coming down the street. I make a run for it. Mom and Jim are sitting in the restaurant window, but neither of them looks my way. I jump on the bus, pay my fare, and settle way in the back. I can see the two of them perfectly from where I am. Mom and Jim are holding hands under the table and talking with their faces close together. The light changes, and they get smaller and smaller as the bus heads west, toward the ocean, toward the red setting sun.

I get off the bus when it turns onto Ocean Avenue and start walking north. I decide to head down the hill to my old neighborhood. I make a left on Mabery Road and walk the long block home. I used to walk this way in fourth and fifth grades and know every tree and gate and dog along the way. Tonight it's on the quiet side. Just a few cars coming and going and that yappy cocker spaniel in the yard of the blue Cape Cod house. As I round the corner onto Ocean Way, my heart starts beating wildly, like I'm trespassing or something, even though I lived here for seven years.

There are no lights on at the house (Mom told me nobody's moved in yet), but it looks on fire from the sunset over the ocean. It's so beautiful—pinks and purples with streaks of crimson like veins running through it. How many times did Mom call me to the balcony or the front yard to watch a great sunset? Or to see the full moon or an orange sliver of one that made the whole sea gleam? How many times did I ignore her? Why didn't I realize what I had until it was gone?

I push open the gate and climb the four brick steps to the front yard. Everything is overgrown. The jasmine bushes my mother planted are raggedy-looking and giving off a sweet perfume. They must think it's spring already, with the recent rains and unseasonably warm weather. Two hummingbirds dive in and out of the bougainvillea. A family of five of them live here, tiny and iridescent green with dabs of pink at their throats. Mostly, they're around early in the morning or at dusk, their feeding times. I wonder what they do with themselves the rest of the day.

Three palm trees line the hibiscus hedge. Two of them grow together from the same trunk, like Siamese twins. I wedge myself between them and stare at the ocean. This was my lookout perch for years. From here, I imagined spotting an invasion from the Far East—although I could never figure out who'd invade us. But I knew I'd become a national hero, have dinner at the White House, hold a press conference. Dozens of birds fly past me at eye level on account of my house being on a bluff. Today I can see up to Malibu and down to the Palos Verdes peninsula and way out to Catalina.

Mom said that she's disappointed we had to move. But she also said that she tries not to get attached to material things. Her parents used to live on a cattle ranch in Cuba, and it was taken away from them when the Communists came to power. This meant they had to leave the country with whatever cash they had on hand and a couple of suitcases. But to me, our house is not just an empty house, a nothing husk. It's where I grew up, where all my memories are buried.

Where do memories go, anyway? Mom says we carry them inside us, that nobody can take them away. But I worry that they'll evaporate like puddles on a hot day. Where's my old self now? Will I need a guide to my past like someone visiting a foreign country? Do exiles feel like this? How am I supposed to remember everything without reminders all around? Mom's already thrown away so much of my stuff, I don't even know what I've lost. Plus, she's forced me to give up things I loved: stuffed animals she donated to charity; books she sent to my aunt's elementary school in New York.

It's not fair.

I try the front door, but it's locked. The windows are dirty and spattered with bird poop, but I can still see inside: the built-in bookcases, the stone fireplace with the Mayan hieroglyphics, the archway to the dining room, the stairs with the wrought-iron banister leading to the second floor. I remember where everything used to be—the paintings and photographs, the sofas and lamps and rugs, and the books, books, books. The Christmas tree used to go in the corner to the right of the fireplace. Will the next family put it there too? How could everything be gone? Mom said she had to get rid of so much because our house in Napa is one third this size. She jokes that it's like trying to fit a size 20 woman into a size 8 dress. I don't find this funny at all.

It shouldn't be too hard to get in around the back. Mom was always forgetting her keys and used to climb along the side of the house and squeeze past the bamboo trees that separated us from our Chinese billionaire neighbor. So that's what I do now, unloosing clumps of dust. I feel like I'm going to choke, but I grit my teeth and keep going. The backyard is in worse condition than the front. The pool is totally congested with weeds and algae and looks like a forgotten pond. The orange trees are heavy with rotting fruit, and there are big rust marks on the patio where our outdoor furniture used to be.

One summer Mom got a book called *A Guide to Backyard Birds* and we started identifying every bird we saw. We counted thirty-seven that July alone. My favorites were the mourning doves. I loved their cooing and the way their wings softly whirred when they took flight. The scrub jays were my least favorite because they killed the mourning doves' baby chicks. Every year the doves hopefully built a nest and laid an egg or two, and every year the scrub jays attacked them. It was terrible. Ducks used to land in our pool every spring, and a couple of times we saw raccoons and once a baby deer. There were too many prowling cats to count.

Who will witness this anymore?

I spot an old pair of goggles near the pool, and it makes me so sad I want to cry again. I taught Véronique how to swim in this pool. My last big birthday party was here and every birthday for the previous seven years. We'd have a pool party and pizza, and then my parents would take me and my friends to the movies in our pajamas and let us order whatever we wanted. Afterward, we'd go home and set up our tents and sleeping bags and watch more movies until everyone fell asleep. In the mornings Mom would serve us bagels and cream cheese until, one by one, my friends' parents came and picked them up. For weeks we'd find strange underwear and clothes tucked into every corner of the house.

The back door to the kitchen is locked, but the window to the den isn't. I slide it open, climb over a jasmine bush, and tumble in. It's strange being here with it empty like this. I mean, it's familiar but strange at the same time, and I'm not sure I belong anymore. It's getting dark, and I'm scared because none of the lights are working. The house smells mildewy. The floorboards are buckling and fungus-ridden where the water leaks through the roof. The fungus looks pink and shiny, like a bright disease. Mom used to say that we could sue the owner for renting us a health hazard, that it was a Third World house in a million-dollar location.

I go upstairs to my room. The remains of a few stickers still decorate my door, though I can hardly make them out. My room is painted lavender, and I can tell by the darker areas where my posters used to be: Matt Dillon and Johnny Depp, the Outsiders, Bob Marley, the Ramones, all the surfers. I want to memorize everything in exact detail. Does my room miss me? Does it remember me playing clarinet? Or the sound of the sea lulling me to sleep? Or that on stormy nights the windows blew open and scared me half to death? Or how I used to call my mom to tuck me in one last time? Or that I begged her not to go away on her lecture trips? Or to read me another poem? Or that Véronique once kissed me on the lips?

A part of me wants to curl up in my old armchair or settle on the floor with my comfy blanket and go to sleep. Suddenly, I'm feeling so tired, like my eyelids are made of lead or something. I open the window to the balcony and climb out. It's windy, and some bad disco music drifts up from the members-only club on the beach. They're probably having a Valentine's Day party. Every New Year's and Fourth of July they shoot off the best fireworks, and we'd get to see them from our house, like it was our own private showing.

The day is nearly gone except for a thin strip of light on the horizon. Then *poof!* It's over. I think about what Mr. Dentini said in science class today. How we're spinning 14 miles a minute around the axis of the earth, 1,080 miles a minute in orbit around the sun. How we're never really standing still. It makes sense to me, and then it doesn't make sense at all. I start worrying about my mom worrying. I've never run away before, and she must be frantic. Once when I was about six, Mom lost me at the farmer's market. When she found me again three minutes later, she burst into tears. By then she'd alerted the National Guard.

It starts to rain, big fat drops that cool my face. I hadn't realized I was feeling so hot. Maybe I'll get a fever and skip school for the rest of the week. Just as I'm trying to decide what to do next, a police car pulls up to the front of the house, sirens blaring. Two officers get out, and one of them has a megaphone. A helicopter drones overhead, but I can't imagine it's for me. Then, just like in the movies, the policeman orders: "Come out with your hands up!"

So, Yumi girl, today's a big day! Going to the racetrack with your old Saul, eh? I'm gonna teach you a thing or two. You never know when a day at the racetrack might come in handy, put a little change in your pocket. Never hurt no one. Hiroko wasn't too happy about me taking you to the track today. But who's gonna argue with a dying man? When I told her it was my last request, she couldn't say nothing. Look around you, kid. It's a sunny day, and the grass is green, and them swans over there just prettify the place, don't you think?

Yeah, I heard you got a rap sheet, heh-heh. Your mother called Hiroko and told her everything. She was afraid you'd try something like that up here. Listen up, Yumi girl, there's no use running away from your problems. 'Cause where are you gonna run to? There'll be up times and down times, and sometimes, looking back, they're the opposite of what you thought. Sometimes big changes force you to grow in ways you can't predict. But if you got a problem, look it straight in the eye and deal. That's good advice, kid. Take it. I wish I'd followed it myself. You can't return to the past, as much as you'd like to. Look at me: I couldn't go back to Japan, and when I finally returned to New York, it didn't work out neither. You gotta keep looking forward, little one. Live in the present; take on the future. That's what I say.

Okay, so you lost some time and money. But didn't the principal promise you another date? Well, you have that much more time to give them a concert nobody will ever forget. Here's ten bucks. Put me down for a couple of tickets. Hiroko and I will be there—you can count on it. Of course we'll make it. I'll be in the front row. Now you go and give it your best shot. That's my girl!

So look here. Santa Anita is one of the great old racetracks—still first-rate. Did you know all the movies stars used to come out here in the forties and fifties? Cary Grant, Carole Lombard, Spencer Tracy, you name it. Not to mention the hoi polloi from Pasadena. Years ago on a beautiful Sunday with a big-stakes race, the stands would be filled to capacity. I'm talking sixty thousand people. It was a sight to see, let me tell you. The crowds today ain't nothing compared to that. Computers and offtrack betting have ruined everything. Now only old-timers like me still come to the track.

In my day I'd pick up the daily racing sheet and study it religiously the night before. Then I'd show up at the track at six or seven to watch the morning workout. I wanted to see the horses for myself. Took your dad to Hollywood Park a lot as a kid. It was only a few miles from our apartment, and we'd go on the bus. Austin loved it there.

I was a pretty good handicapper, if I do say so myself. I could usually dope out the two or three horses in contention. My main problem—this is according to your dad, who thinks he knows everything—is that I'd sabotage myself with my betting. The fact is, I never bet favorites. Me, I was always looking for a horse to beat the favorite. Because the greater the odds, the bigger the payoff, Yumi girl. That's what taking risks is all about. I lost a lot of money that way, but when I won, I won big. That's still the way to go, in my opinion. Anything else is for chumps. Why do you think they call it "chump change"?

Now the two most important things to remember in horse racing are class and consistency. You're gonna get sick of me saying this. Like today we're at a stakes race, which is the best level of competition. But there are two other levels—allowance races and claiming races.

You're confused? Maybe I'm going a little too fast. Here's what I really think about the track, Yumi girl, what it can teach you, what it's taught me. You win some and you lose some, but you gotta keep your cool either way. It's called "grace under pressure," and it's the mark of a true gentleman. This goes for the ladies, too. In my opinion, you can learn everything you need to learn about someone by watching him win and watching him lose. That's where character will show through. It's not that the tracks make a man, but they'll sure reveal him. And that's something worth knowing, little one. You following me?

Here, I'm gonna stake you twenty bucks. There are nine races today, so you can bet two or three dollars a race. Or break it up any way you want. What? You want to bet it all on the Tin Man? You're telling me you're gonna risk it all on one horse because you like his name? Heh-heh. You're funny, little one. Stubborn, too. Okay, okay, it's your money. See here, don't you want to take a look at any of these other horses? Milk It Mick? Or Rebel Rebel? What about Adreamisborn? I know it's a corny name, but you gotta look at the statistics.

Sometimes you remind me of your father, Yumi. He loved to bet on the come-from-behind horses. They could be dead last for a mile and then they'd start charging for the finish line. Those horses could really fly! I don't know how long he stayed glued to the TV watching replays of Secretariat at the Belmont Stakes. It was a thing of beauty, that horse. A mile and a half in two minutes and twenty-four seconds flat. Thirty-one lengths ahead of the next closest horse. Shattered every record. Your dad was twelve years old. It was the last time Austin was so happy, he hugged me. Yeah, he hugged me for all he was worth.

Well, okay, I'll keep telling you my story but only in between the races. They last just a minute or two, but there's nothing more exciting in the world, if you ask me. "And they're off!" . . . the three sweetest words in the English language! We get a half hour between races to figure out what to bet next. You sure you wanna put all your money on the Tin Man? So you're an expert already? All right, I'll leave it alone.

I'm not sure there's all that much more to tell. After your dad was born, Hiroko went to work every day and I stayed home with

Austin. Nowadays it's fashionable to talk about househusbands and whatnot, but in those days it was shameful. But I tried to make my peace with it. Did the best I could. Figured I could at least try to be more of a father than my own father was to me. I owed Austin that much. It wasn't how I thought my life would turn out, but it was the hand I was dealt, and I dealt with it the best I could.

Basically, I took care of your dad and made sure he had enough to eat. Never was much of a cook, but I made him a peanut butter sandwich and a cup of coffee and we'd be off to the park or to check out some hippie demonstration (there were lots of those in the sixties). And I'd talk to him about politics, events of the day. The kid was well informed. We went to the racetrack a couple times a week. Austin grew up at the tracks. That was an education in itself. Everybody knew him there, rubbed his head for good luck. I got some ribbin' from the regulars about having my kid tag along, but soon nobody cared no more.

The years went by fast when I look back on them. Before you know it, Austin was halfway through grade school. He was a good student. Must've been all that fish Hiroko ate when she was pregnant. Austin started reading like nobody's business. He was analyzing the racing sheets when he was four. Fighting with me over the Los Angeles Times when he was five. It got so I had to let him have the sports section first thing every morning or he'd throw a fit. Basketball was his sport. He was a little guy, but it didn't stop him from trying to muscle in on the games at the park. Decent outside shooter too.

From the get-go, Austin never wanted help from nobody. Insisted on doing everything himself. That was the kind of kid he was. Proud and stubborn, just like you. He wouldn't take no for an answer neither. That was the hard part because we had to say no to him a lot. Money was tight, and we couldn't buy him the things he wanted, things other kids had. He had to wait a whole year for his first bicycle. Never could afford to pay for music lessons, and he begged us for them. It hurts me to say this now.

All the while, Hiroko was working at the factory. Working, working, working. We hardly saw her. We were living in a one-bedroom apartment down from Piñeda's Mexican restaurant. Me and Hiroko slept on a pullout couch in the living room so Austin could have his own room. No matter how much I told her not to or tried to help, when Hiroko got home every night, she'd start cooking and cleaning until long after me and Austin went to bed. Like I said, the woman don't sleep.

Anyway, I raised Austin as best I could. I went to the school meetings with the other mothers. I met with his teachers (they thought I was his grandfather) and took him to the library on Friday afternoons. I did what I had to do. If more men did this, believe me, they wouldn't have no time to go to war. One Christmas, I got some seasonal work at the post office, but then I couldn't pick Austin up after school and he was home alone until five thirty. That just about broke my heart.

Would I've rather been doing something else? Sometimes I thought so. On the worst days I resented being home with Austin,

CRISTINA GARCÍA

having no freedom to do what I wanted. I suffered some serious cabin fever now and then. You gotta remember I was in my fifties by then and I'd spent my whole life living it my way. But I stuck it out and I'm glad I did. Few men get to do what I did. Hey, as far as I know, I might be the only guy of my generation to do it.

The truth is, raising a child humbles you like nothing else in the world. But you know what, Yumi girl? I'd do it again in a heartbeat. I'm prouder of raising your dad than I am of anything else I've done. And that's the honest truth. I only wish me and your dad could be pals the way we were when he was little. I ain't sure what went wrong. But after that Secretariat race, he never hugged me again.

Your race is up next, Yumi girl. Let's go to the window, okay? You heard it right. Yep, that's what the girl said. Twenty dollars on the Tin Man.

I'M STANDING IN FRONT OF MAYBE 70 PERCENT OF THE orchestra, trying to whip them into shape for our April Fools' Day concert. It's less than two weeks away, but all the energy seems to have gone out of our rehearsals.

"Who's to say Mr. Minor won't cancel our concert again?" Zoë complains, setting down her bassoon.

"Look, we've been through this before," I say. "He's written out a contract for us. He's signed it. I have it right here."

"So what are we going to do if he doesn't comply?" the trombonist shouts. "Take him to court?"

"Off with his head!" Alex Pavel declares dramatically, making a guillotine motion with his cello bow.

This gets everybody giggling and speculating about suing Mr. Minor, imagining him behind bars in striped pajamas.

I'm getting discouraged by the lack of concentration. I thought having an extra six weeks to practice would make our orchestra sound better, not worse. But nothing doing. Something's been lost, and I don't know how to get it back.

Mom and I are supposed to take a red-eye to New York tonight for a long weekend. We're going to see Tía Paloma and Isabel, who are finally back from Guatemala. It can't come soon enough for me. Saul's been telling me not to give up, to go after what I want and not settle for less. But what if what you want depends on the cooperation of sixty-three other people who aren't as determined or enthusiastic as you?

"Maybe we should just forget it," Lucy Kim says.

"We're fooling ourselves," a violist mutters.

"We sound worse than we did *before* Valentine's Day!" These are the trumpeters complaining from the back row.

"I mean, what's the point?" Kara insists. "We're all graduating in a couple of months anyway. Do we really care what happens after we leave?"

"Yeah, but we still have to do this," I try to counter. "Aren't we artists?"

I look over at Eli, but he doesn't even have the decency to make his usual obscene noise on the tuba. Apathy reigns, and I'm supposed to be conducting it. I shoot Squid-boy a help-me-out-here look, but he shrugs his shoulders like there's nothing we can do anymore. I'm at the end of my rope. We have ten minutes of rehearsal left. What can I say to motivate them again? To instill in them how important this is, if not for us, then for everyone who's coming after us? Should I simply let everyone go home?

Just then Mom shows up in the back of the auditorium with a huge tray of fudge brownies. Everyone drops their instruments and descends on her, grabbing two and three at a time. Jim is with her, grinning like a fool and trying to be nice to everyone. He flies in from Texas practically every other week now. It's so annoying. Plus, I don't want anyone thinking he's my dad. Mom looks up at me and gets the picture pretty fast. My face is misery personified.

"Now listen up, everyone," she begins in a stronger-than-usual New York accent. "I've brought a very special guest today."

I can see her wheels turning, and suddenly, I'm totally in sync with her. But can I really go through with this? Doesn't it make me a collaborator?

"His name is Jim Holman," I add, tentatively, "and he is a real orchestra conductor from Austin, Texas. We've asked him here today so that he can listen to us and make suggestions. He runs a youth symphony festival every summer and might even invite us, depending on our performance today."

Jim is looking completely perplexed, turning to my mother with his eyes open wide.

"Mr. Holman, are you ready?" I ask in the most professional-sounding voice I can muster.

The orchestra is in a state of shock, half-eaten brownies in their mouths. This is a surprise nobody expected, not even me!

"Everyone, please take your places," I announce, and they scurry into position, hurriedly swallowing their brownies. Maybe we should've distributed a little milk before continuing. Their mouths have probably gone dry.

I take the podium and glance over to a still-stunned-looking Jim. But from the very first note, I can tell the orchestra is alive again. "Anarchy in the U.K." sounds pretty good for a change. Quincy is thumping away on his double bass and does a killer solo. The violins, including the recently skeptical Lucy Kim, are playing with more gusto than I've heard in a month. I can hear Mom swaying to the music from her squeaky third-row seat. She's probably enjoying this more than anyone. The trumpets finally get it together and blast away with only a couple of sour notes. They're such showmen anyway. They only need an audience to rise to the occasion. Why does it always take an outsider to galvanize us to do our best?

When I lower my baton after the final chorus, everyone is flushed with excitement but totally silent. It's time to hear the verdict. Jim looks in my direction. He doesn't seem the least bit fazed by the punk music. This is a man who spends his life with Bach and Beethoven, not Sid Vicious. I'm impressed.

"First, I want to thank Yumi Ruíz-Hirsch for inviting me here today," he says. "She is as dedicated an orchestra director as I've ever seen."

To my utter shock, everyone thunderously stomps their feet in approval. I feel my face get hot with embarrassment.

"Secondly, I would like to extend a formal invitation to the Wilton Middle School orchestra to attend the Fourth Annual Youth Symphony Festival in Austin, Texas, this July. We need a group that can play for the big dance."

There's a moment of disbelief. Alex drops his bow in the silence. Finally, Eli blows an obscene noise through his tuba, and the cheering and mayhem begin.

"Now, I have just a few minor suggestions," Jim begins over the merriment. "If you're going to play punk, let's get those bows closer to the bridge. . . ."

Okay, maybe everything's going to be all right after all.

I'm still thinking this as our plane makes its way down the runway, then climbs into the night sky. Mom and I will be in New York first thing in the morning and will stay for three days. This means no school for me on Monday and—if Mom takes pity on me—maybe Tuesday, too. We're going to New York for two reasons: to see an off-off-Broadway theater adaptation of my mom's first novel, *Coconut Flan*; and to attend baby Isabel's christening. Tía Paloma asked me to play the clarinet at the ceremony, which is in a church. Abuela and Gramps are coming up from Miami, and cousins I've never even heard of are converging for the festivities.

My mom is reading poetry in the window seat next to me. I give her about six minutes before she's sound asleep. She encourages me to read, but I feel too antsy. So instead, she recites something from the book in her hands:

I sat down
inside a pause in time.
In a still pool
of silence:
a formidable ring,
where bright stars
crashed into the twelve black,
floating numerals.

Mom takes my hand and kisses me good night. "It's good we're getting away for a little while, *mi amor*," she murmurs sleepily. "You've been working so hard. Now you can spend some time with the other half of the family, with your Cuban side." Then she falls asleep, snoring softly against her little airline pillow.

I look out the window at the darkness, my mom's hand still warm in mine. I think about how easy it would be for me not to exist. What if my parents had never met? Would I still be out in the universe somewhere, waiting to be called down to

CRISTINA GARCÍA

earth? Or be part of a star or a speck of cosmic dust? Mom says nearly everything boils down to chance and leaps of faith. Not even scientists really know how we came to be. There are lots of theories, of course, but nobody knows absolutely for sure.

Saul said it best, I think: *I'd rather live with uncertainty than believe easy answers, only to have something to believe in.* That sounds about right to me. These past few months he's talked to me more than I've ever heard him talk before. If I hadn't specifically asked him to tell me his story, I'd still be in the dark about his life. Plus, I wouldn't have learned so much about mine, either.

I put on my headset and flip through the stations. I settle on the weather channel, chuckling about Jim's preoccupation with cloud formations. I pick up my mom's poetry book and start turning the pages to find an image I like, but nothing jumps out at me. I'm getting drowsy and cuddle next to her. I try to forget everything that's been bothering me lately and just be. Mom puts her arm around me, still half asleep, and I finally nod off.

The next thing I know, we're landing in New York. I'm fuzzy with exhaustion and my neck aches from lying sidewise half the night. I had another one of my owl dreams, except this time the owl stared at me without saying anything. Very creepy. In the airport Mom is all business—luggage, cabs, umbrellas, not forgetting this or that. I hate it when she's more awake than I am and rushing, rushing, rushing, which is practically every minute lately.

I miss my dad all of a sudden and call him on my new cell phone (Mom relented and got me one two weeks ago). It's four in the morning in L.A., so I know he's awake, but I get his answering machine. He's changed the message to him singing from the middle of "I Wanna Be Your Shoebox":

I WANNA BE YOUR SOAP BOX
I WANNA BE YOUR BOBBY SOX
I WANNA BE YOUR RED FOX
I WANNA BE YOUR BAGELS AND LOX

YEAH, YEAH, BABY, LET ME BE YOUR SHOEBOX
LET ME BE YOUR SWEET SHOEBOX

His voice sounds sad and lonely. I worry about my dad when I go away. When I'm there, at least he has to get out of bed, take me to school, make sure I eat. My presence gives him structure, however flimsy that structure is. I'm not sure he'd get out of bed just to tune a piano or two, no matter how much money he got paid. Dad isn't motivated by money. Mostly, I think this is a good thing. But then again, I have a mother who takes care of that stuff. I've never gone hungry or had to fret over having enough money to buy a yearbook, or clothes, or anything like that.

Mom is arguing with the cabdriver over the route he's taking to Tía Paloma's house in Brooklyn. She threatens to cut ten dollars off the fare because he took the Belt Parkway instead of the Long Island Expressway. (Nobody calls freeways "freeways" here.) The driver must know she's dangerous because, to my surprise, he gives in. We drive along the coast a lot of the way, and it's pretty, though not great for surfing. It's overcast, and the sky and the sea are a million shades of gray. Seagulls hover over the dunes, and a huge flock of birds—Mom thinks they're Canadian geese—fly north, flapping for all they're worth.

Tía Paloma is excited to see us and ushers us into her third-floor apartment. She's laid out a big breakfast: three kinds of cereal, pineapple juice, a platter of assorted bagels, butter, cream cheese, smoked salmon with capers, scrambled eggs, multiple jars of marmalade, and a big bowl of fruit salad. Isabel wakes up with the commotion, and we rush to her crib, which is crowded with stuffed animals.

She looks enormous to me, triple the size she was in Guatemala. Tía Paloma must be feeding her nonstop. Isabel has these thick black eyebrows too, like the self-portraits of Frida Kahlo I saw at the L.A. County Museum last year. Her eyelids are so soft-looking, you can see the faint blue capillaries under her skin. Isabel is confused to see strangers in her room and starts crying. She clings to Tía Paloma and shakes her black curls. I want to take her in my arms and say,

It's gonna be okay, little one. We're your new family now. You can trust us.

Mom gets down on the floor, picks up a toy giraffe, and tells Isabel a made-up story about its life back in Africa. Soon Isabel is crawling all over her and giving her more stuffed animals for the story. I'm enlisted to be a penguin visiting from Antarctica. First, I try a deep-sounding voice that upsets Isabel, so I change to a squeaky, happy voice. This makes her laugh, and she claps her hands and wants me to keep talking. When Isabel throws her arms around my neck, I melt into squeaky happiness.

After breakfast Mom and I settle into the daybed in Isabel's room for a nap, but Isabel keeps waking us up every five minutes to play. Finally, her babysitter arrives to take her to the park, and Tía Paloma goes off to run errands for the christening party. She promises to meet up with us at the theater later that night.

Don't ask me how it happened, but at two o'clock that afternoon I'm with my Cuban grandmother at some ultrafancy hairdresser's on Fifth Avenue. After lunch Mom decided to go museum hopping (not my favorite activity), and Abuela somehow persuaded me to get my hair cut and styled for the theater premiere tonight. The hairdresser is thin as a knife and dressed in head-to-toe black, the New York uniform. His name is Anthony, and the first thing he says when Abuela introduces us is: "Oh, dear girl! No, no, no, no, no, no, no!" I might've missed a "no" or two. This doesn't sound too promising.

I'm not stuck-up about my looks, but I do have pretty nice hair. People in L.A. compliment me on it all the time. My mother's one fashionable friend—the vegan fanatic—is constantly telling me not to cut it. My hair is wavy, sun-streaked, and nearly down to my waist. Okay, so it's a little dry and I have a few split ends. (Mom swats my hands away every time I mess with them.) No big deal, right? Well, by the time Anthony double shampoos it, triple conditions it, cracks an egg into it, applies foul-smelling gunk on it, trims it, blow-dries it, and immobilizes it with hair spray, I no longer recognize myself. In fact, I look like a fugitive from Big Hair Planet.

Abuela is cooing and fussing and telling me how gorgeous I look, and everyone in the beauty salon comes around oohing and aahing at my transformation, and nobody—not one single person—bothers to ask me what I think. I'm wondering where I could buy a blowtorch and do away with my hair altogether when Abuela air kisses her way out of the salon and we head over to Saks. She's promised to buy me an outfit to go with my great new look. Like what would that be? An aluminum space suit?

We travel up, up, up what seems to be the longest escalator in North America and enter a world of taffeta and chiffon, satins, silks, and lace. We're talking Pouf City here. Still in a trance, I'm led into an enormous fitting room with soft lighting and mirrors. I take off my California clothes—ripped jeans with a patterned skirt over them, my favorite black and red Clash T-shirt, and my torn-up sneakers with the squids Quincy drew on them when he still liked me. I find myself trying on a series of dresses that make me look like I got caught in a cotton candy machine.

Who wears this stuff, anyway? Abuela chirps on about debutante balls and *quinceañeras* and the parties they used to have in prerevolutionary Cuba "before that tyrant hijacked the country and ground it to dust." But I'm hardly listening. I shuffle out of the fitting room in a dress that makes me look like Princess Barbie. Abuela pronounces it *perfecto!* Before I can protest, she buys it, along with some Cinderella-like slippers and sparkly panty hose (something I've never worn in my entire life—we go bare-legged in L.A., even in winter). It occurs to her that she has a camera in that bottomless handbag of hers, and she begs me to let her take a picture of "the new you." I try to muster what's left of my former self and shake my head.

"*Por favor, mi amor,*"Abuela pleads. "Just one little picture, to show my friends in Miami. I want them to see what a beautiful granddaughter I have."

"No," I whisper.

Abuela holds up the camera and starts fiddling with the flash.

"No," I say a little louder, shaking my head.

CRISTINA GARCÍA

She holds up the camera and takes aim, smiling at me and displaying her perfectly bleached teeth.

"No!" I scream, and knock the camera out of her hands.

Okay, so that didn't go too well. I'm back in my own clothes for the theater performance and keeping my distance from Abuela, who manages to look hurt and proud and pathetic all at the same time. I've apologized to her a million times, but it doesn't seem to be enough. Mom is furious at me for "resorting to violence," as she puts it, even if it was in self-defense. You see, the camera fell on one of my grandmother's hammertoes and broke it. She ended up in the emergency room and has a big, ostentatious bandage on her foot. She's lied to everyone except my mom and Gramps, saying that *she* dropped the camera on her foot, all the while casting baleful looks in my direction. Is this what "guilty" feels like?

The play is about to start, and there's this great welcome for my mother. The audience is excited that she's here on opening night. It's weird to think of my mom as famous in any way. When I was little, I wanted to be like her and wrote paragraph-long stories about quirky characters. I remember one about a guy who walked funny, and then the whole neighborhood started walking funny too.

Coconut Flan is a one-woman show starring this Peruvian-Swedish actress with long, wavy hair. I reach for my own hair, shorn to my shoulders and still sticky with hair spray. The actress is playing the four main characters in the book, but mostly, she talks in the voice of Yoli, the youngest of a crazy clan of Cuban women. I start getting self-conscious because the name Yoli sounds so similar to Yumi, and I'm afraid everyone's going to think the character is me. I mean, Yoli loves punk music like I do, argues with her mother like I do, has a serious attitude like I do.

Mom must be reading my mind because she whispers in my ear: "Don't worry, Yumi. Nobody's going to think it's you. This happened in the seventies, and if anything, Yoli is *my* alter ego."

Still, I feel like I want to bolt from the theater, but I'm trapped in the front row. Besides, how would it look for the author's own daughter to run screaming for the exit? I close my eyes and try not to listen. I can hear the audience laughing, even Abuela and Tía Paloma and all the cousins. I wonder why I'm the only one having trouble with this when I realize: *It's not their mother!* None of them would so much as smirk if it were their own mother's words blaring back at them.

Mercifully, it's only a one-act play. The actress gets a standing ovation, and then the audience clamors for my mom to take a bow. She does so, reluctantly, and invites me to go on stage with her. A question-and-answer period follows. People ask my mom about her characters, her inspiration, her work process. She's funny and charming, and people seem to like her. It's strange to see her in this light. After all, to me, she's just my mom, but to other people, she's something else entirely: a real writer, someone to ask questions of, a person to admire. I'm very relieved when Mom makes a point of saying that the Yoli character has nothing to do with her own daughter—thanks, Mom! Then: "Does anyone have questions for Yumi?"

At first I'm mortified, but people seem genuinely interested in me, too. I tell them how much I love punk music, that I play the clarinet and surf in Venice, and that I hope to go to college in New York someday. Shyly, I tell them about the fund-raising concert I'm organizing for our orchestra and that my grandfather, Saul, is the inspiration for most of what I do. I want to tell them about Quincy, too, but I already feel like I'm going overboard, so I stop. In answer to a question from an old lady in the back row, I say: "I'm not sure what I want to be when I grow up, but I played the Ouija board once with my best friend, Véronique, and it said I was going to be an editor." Everyone laughs really hard at this and starts applauding like I'm some kind of genius. Hmmmm, I like how this feels. Yeah, I like how this feels a lot.

The next day is Isabel's christening, and everyone is gathered at a church in Brooklyn for the ceremony. Abuela and Tiá Paloma are dressed in silk suits—Abuela's is pale peach with an elaborate hat; Tía Paloma's is sea foam green with matching pumps. But the star of the proceedings is Isabel herself in a lacy gown that makes her look like a nineteenth-century doll.

Saul has a photograph of himself looking just like Isabel does today, except that in his day babies wore these kinds of gowns all the time. Isabel has on this cute bonnet she keeps pulling off her head. Abuela patiently puts it back on and triple knots it, but Isabel finds a way to pull it off again. I'm feeling this intense solidarity with her. *Go, girl!* I want to shout out, but I keep my mouth shut for a change.

The priest doesn't move his lips when he speaks, but his voice comes out strong and powerful, like he's a ventriloquist or something. It's hard for me to follow, but everyone is muttering "Amen" and "Praise be the Lord" throughout. There's incense and a marble basin filled with water. Isabel's bonnet comes off for good, and the priest pours water on her forehead and rubs it with oils. My mom, who's the godmother (Tía Paloma didn't pick a godfather), repeats the vows after the priest, and it's done.

Tía Paloma nods to me, which means it's time for me to play my clarinet. I chose the second movement from Mozart's first clarinet concerto. It's so beautiful and airy and complicated all at once. It sounds like a celebration (almost all of Mozart does). I begin the piece, and the notes reverberate off the walls of the church and the stained-glass windows and float up to the ceiling before echoing back in an awesome circle of sound. Everyone stands very still listening to it. My tone is perfect, and I don't even think about my breathing, and my fingers seem to move on their own. It's the best I've ever played. When I finish, I understand

CRISTINA GARCÍA

that I belong here, too, with my mom and her family. As much as I belong with Saul and Hiroko and my dad.

∞∞

So the first thing you gotta remember about poker, Yumi girl, is that it's a zero-sum game. If you win, someone else loses, and vice versa. Winning is a lot more fun, believe me. But you gotta know when to fold. It's all about the odds. You're not good at math? This ain't rocket science we're talking about here. You never know when it might come in handy. Didn't you win a nice piece of change at the racetrack? I know you didn't follow my advice, heh-heh. That's the mark of a maverick! But you gotta learn the rules in order to break them, right? Look, you need three things to win at poker: a first-rate memory, the ability to read people, and heart. That means the courage to bet the farm when the odds are in your favor. Don't hold back. Nobody gets ahead pussyfootin' around.

Yeah, I'm glad to hear the orchestra is getting back on track. I knew you could do it, kid. I ain't right about everything, but I know a tough cookie when I see one. So have you decided on the final songs yet? What? It's a surprise? A big surprise? No kidding. You sure are something. Never was one for surprises, but I guess I have no choice in the matter, eh?

Now let's deal. What? A good luck charm? You're my good luck charm, little one. I never would've lasted this long without you. You want something of mine for good luck? Well, I ain't got no locks of hair to give you, heh-heh. My gold watch? I'll tell you what—you can have it once I kick the bucket. Hiroko! I want you to give Yumi here my watch when I'm gone, okay? How's about I give you this little jade Buddha in the meanwhile? Got it in Japan years ago. Kept it in my pocket when my horses raced. Go ahead, take it. Bring it with you to college. Put it on your wedding cake.

Listen to your grandmother, Yumi. Always fussing, trying to get me to eat something. "C'mon, Daddy, eat, eat," like I'm some kid. I can't stand it no more. I used to enjoy a good steak and a baked potato, you know? A hunk of rye bread on the side. But I can't taste nothing no more. Might as well be putting sawdust in my mouth. Look how she vacuums around me like I'm a piece of furniture. It's undignified is what it is. Now you want to give me a shave? Me and Yumi are trying to play some poker here. You see how she treats me? She don't listen to nothing I say.

Never a day's peace around here. You don't mind, do you, kid? Your grandmother still likes to shave me once a week. Used to be every day, but my whiskers are slow to grow now. Clips my nails too. I know she's taking good care of me, but there's such a thing as overdoing it. Haven't you heard the expression "Let old dogs lie"? Well, I'm an old dog and I want to lie.

There's so many things people do again and again—and for what? It's like a traffic light turning red, then green, then red again. Stop, go, stop, go, until it makes you dizzy to think about it. It's the same pointless stuff. Look, I wish I could pass on some great truth to you, Yumi girl. I wish I could say I discovered something that if I told you would save you time and heartbreak. But only experience teaches you lessons that stick.

Well, I don't know what more there is to tell. The years piled up on top of one another. I looked after your dad. Went to the track. Kept up with the news. I wish you'd been around for the civil rights movement. That was something to see. Or Neil Armstrong walking on the moon. Or Secretariat at Belmont. Or cheered with me when that bum President Nixon got impeached. That's right, I watched the news and went to the tracks and tried to raise your dad right.

So that's about it. The years flew by is what I'm saying. Hiroko worked and cleaned and cooked. After a couple of years she saved enough money to buy a secondhand Toyota. Oh, she was proud of that old thing. Kept it shiny and changed the oil herself every two thousand miles. Me, I never could get used to driving again. I took the test in California and failed. Hey, I'm from Brooklyn, remember? We walk everywhere or take the subway or the bus. It's no big deal.

As I was saying, your grandmother loved that car of hers. Once in a while she'd drive us out to San Pedro to watch the hustle and bustle of the port. Reminded me of when I was a kid and hanging around the Brooklyn docks. I loved to see those giant cranes unloading the boxcars from Hong Kong and Japan. Today most of the imports come from China. It's the new superpower, you know.

Back then Hiroko would drive Austin to the airport sometimes to meet the Lakers after they'd played out of town. Never seen a bigger basketball fan than your dad. Tickets were reasonable then, but we couldn't afford to go to a game but once a season. Hiroko would make a special dinner: steak for me; curry rice for her and your dad. Then Austin would put on his Lakers jersey and we'd drive over to the arena listening to the pregame talk on the radio.

We stayed in Hawthorne all those years but moved from one apartment to another, each one a little better than the last. Hiroko called the shots as far as money was concerned. I didn't like it, but what could I do? When I look back on those years, I get angry with myself. I should've stayed in New York or tried harder to get a job doing something, anything. But I felt old already. I know it sounds silly, but you gotta remember that fifty was considered an old man then. But what's the use of regrets? If I hadn't taken care of your dad, you wouldn't be here, Yumi girl. So everything turned out right in the end.

Even before Austin got to high school, we knew we had a smart kid on our hands. I wonder sometimes if his brains didn't get in his way. He brought home straight A's without trying, but he fell in with the wrong crowd. Started hanging out at the beach with surfers and riffraff. What? No offense intended, Yumi. I ain't saying all surfers are riffraff, but them kids were up to no good. They were into that punk music and wearing chains and safety pins and whatnot. No, I don't want you to play the Ramones for me. You're never gonna convince me. Why don't you put on some Benny Goodman for me instead?

It's a miracle Austin didn't end up in jail or something. It was about then that he stopped talking to us. Thought he knew it all.

CRISTINA GARCÍA

We couldn't say nothing because he was doing good in school and bringing in money working at that record store. But we were lucky to get three words out of him in a day. He stayed out late and wasn't around on the weekends, neither. He forgot we existed. Austin was valedictorian for Hawthorne High, class of '78. He got two full college scholarships: one to Amherst and the other to USC.

Hiroko and I were proud of him, but we talked him into staying in town. We argued that it'd be cheaper for him to live at home, that I was getting old. Twenty-five years ago we were saying that. Little did I know what getting old would really mean. That was our big mistake. He should've gone out in the world, tested himself. Instead, he stayed here and never left. Dropped out of USC after two years and trained himself as a piano tuner. Nothing wrong with tuning pianos. It's honest work. But your dad could've done more with his life.

Talking about all this tires me out, Yumi girl. My breath feels raw inside me. Don't you hear it? I slept until noon today. Most days I sleep twelve, fourteen hours like a newborn baby. What goes around comes around, I guess. Maybe I've been waiting all this time for you to come along—to tell you stories, teach you a few things. Look how well you did at the track. And now you're beating me at poker! How'd all those chips end up on your side of the table, eh?

Whoa, just look at that rain come down! Never used to rain like this in Los Angeles, Yumi girl. Before you were born, it hadn't *rained a drop in five years. People were putting bricks in their toilets, emptying their pools, letting their lawns dry out, showering with their neighbors—heh-heh, just kidding about that one. It was a serious drought. Now with global warming and whatnot, they say we're all going to be underwater in fifty years. Well, I'll be gone by the time that happens, and it's a good thing too. You know I can't swim. Don't tell me it ain't too late to learn. You'll teach me? Okay, if I make it till summer, you'll give me a lesson. That's a deal.*

IT'S HARD TO BELIEVE APRIL FOOLS' DAY IS FINALLY HERE. IT'S been one crisis after another, but—miracle of miracles—the concert is still on for tonight! We've sold 812 tickets at five dollars each (that's $4,060), more than I ever thought possible. Plus, we're expecting lots more people at the door. Quincy has coordinated the bake sale of a thousand butter cookies shaped like musical notes, give or take a few dozen he ate himself. I've done nothing but think, breathe, and dream this concert for the last two weeks. I even donated all the money I made at the racetrack ($140) to buy everyone snazzy red bow ties. Like Saul says, you gotta do things with some heart.

I was so nervous, I could hardly sleep last night. When I did manage a few winks, the owl from my dream was back— except this time it was gigantic. It kept swooping over the orchestra and plucking away people's instruments. First to go was Lucy's violin (carried in its talons by the strings), followed by Kara's flute and Zoë's bassoon. By the end of the dream the owl made off with Eli's tuba and the whole set of timpani! Finally, I woke up in a sweat at five in the morning and couldn't get back to sleep. I decided to go down to the beach and surf to calm my nerves. That's where I am now.

It's been raining like crazy for the past two months, so I haven't been able to surf in ages. The waves have been amazing too, really high and really fast, especially in Malibu. Reports say that it's been the best surfing season in Southern California in ten years and surfers are coming in from all over. The ocean looks kind of scary to me, though. Mom drove me out to Point Dume on Sunday to watch the pros. I wanted so badly to go out, even just to ride the whitewash, but Mom wouldn't let me near the water.

Nobody knows I'm down here today. Dad is fast asleep, and I snuck out without eating a thing because that would've definitely woken up Millie. It's almost six, and there's a light drizzle out. The beach is that light bluish gray color you see before the sun comes out full force. I think it's the prettiest time of all out here. If you ask me, dawn belongs more to the end of the night than the beginning of the day. I love it because it's so indefinite, so in-between that you can't pinpoint the exact moment night surrenders to day.

There isn't a soul on the beach. The ocean is real quiet,

the surf barely a ripple. It's almost as if it were waiting for me, beckoning me, telling me to come on in and relax a little. I paddle way out without much resistance. The ocean smells sweet and fishy at the same time, but I don't mind. I get sprayed in the face as I paddle. The water glimmers in the early sunlight. It's like paddling through liquid emeralds. My feet are freezing, but it's so beautiful that I want to cry.

When I get past the last break, I sit up on my board and enjoy everything around me: the gentle lapping of the waves, the streaks of silver clouds, the soft mound of beach in the distance. To the north of me, the pier sits idle. The Ferris wheel and roller coaster look like artifacts from prehistoric times. It may sound strange to say I feel cozy out here on the ocean, but that's exactly right. I feel at home here, just me and my board adrift on the water. And I know somehow that this will always be here for me, no matter where I end up. Suddenly, I hear splashing behind me, and I spot a school of dolphins heading south. *Dolphin alert!* I can hear my mom calling, waking me up. Except I'm already awake and I saw them first.

School is complete madness. Nobody can concentrate on account of the concert later tonight, and I think I managed to flunk my geometry test. Quincy is all business, checking things off his list. We're supposed to have one last rehearsal before the performance, but he thinks we should cancel it so nobody can overhear us ahead of time.

"Are you sure we're ready enough?" I ask.

"Any readier and we'll stink like a school of mackerel."

We both start cracking up but just as quickly stop.

"So we're on?" Quincy asks, though it sounds more like a command.

He sticks out his hand to shake mine, like we're formalizing a big bank merger or something. I shake his hand back, sheepishly, and force a smile.

"By the way," he adds, "we're down to maybe six hundred butter cookies."

"What happened?"

"Well, a bunch of them broke and . . . I got kind of hungry last night."

"That's all right, don't worry about it," I say, trying not to laugh again. Then I march off to history class.

Will this day never end? Time has never moved so slowly in my life. In the hallways and around school, people are saying hi and waving their tickets at me. There's definitely a sense of anticipation. The pressure starts building in me so badly, I can hardly stand it. I try to calm down, thinking about Saul and Hiroko sitting there in the first row, cheering me on. Saul was the one who encouraged me to keep going when all seemed lost. He told me to be persistent, win or lose. I'm only hoping it won't be a total disaster. Mom and Dad have been pretty encouraging too. "What's the worst that can happen?" Dad teased me. "The orchestra has a meltdown and plays the *William Tell* overture instead?"

The concert is at seven o'clock, but the orchestra is supposed to be there an hour early. Quincy and I get there at four thirty to set up the bake sale and make sure the auditorium is ready—lights, music stands, sound equipment. I've learned something from all this running around. If you want something done, you have to fight to make it happen. Only Quincy is as reliable as I am. When he says he'll do something, he does it. That's better than 99 percent of the people I know. As Saul would say, his word is golden. The only problem is: Who knows if Squid-boy will even talk to me after the concert is over?

The musicians start trickling in a little after six. There's a crisis with Rachel Lehmer, our second cellist. She sprained her wrist and doesn't think she'll be able to play. I tell her to tighten up her Ace bandage and get on stage. Cindy Grady has some kind of lip injury she says she got from biting into an apple and can't play her French horn. From the way she kisses her boyfriend, though, I suspect she'll survive the concert. I simply encourage her to do her best. I keep looking up at the rafters, half expecting to see the owl from my dream. *It was only a dream.* I repeat this to myself like a mantra.

"You're talking to yourself." Squid-boy comes up to me as I'm doing this. "Don't make me worry about you."

By five to seven, the auditorium is packed. There's a huge buzzing sound, like we're trapped in some giant beehive. All the musicians are in their places except for Quincy and me. I keep peeking out from behind the curtains to see if Saul and Hiroko and my parents have arrived. I cordoned off the front row with a RESERVED sign to make sure they'd get good seats. There's no way I want to start the concert without Saul. I want this to be a big thank-you gift to him. A thank-you for everything he's shared with me, for looking out for me and looking forward to seeing me every week. But I know there's no real way I can repay him except to do my best. Yeah, that would make him happy.

At eight minutes after seven, there's still no sign of them.

"We've got to start," Quincy insists, but I can tell he feels bad about it. His dad hasn't shown up either. I don't think his dad has shown up to anything he's done, ever.

"You don't understand!" I whine, even though I think he does.

Just when I'm about to give up on them, I see Saul hobbling down the aisle with Hiroko at his elbow. Dad is behind them, and Mom and Jim are bringing up the rear. I catch Saul's eye as he settles into his seat, and I know I'm ready to go—ready as I'll ever be. Quincy takes his place behind his double bass. The curtains open. There's light applause as I walk over to the conductor's podium and look out at the orchestra with a big smile.

Then I hold up the baton and speak only loud enough for the musicians to hear: "Let's play like the giants we are!"

And we do. Somehow, miraculously, we pull it off. I don't think anybody's ever heard an orchestra like ours play punk and juiced-up reggae. The Sex Pistols, the Ramones, the Clash, Bob Marley and the Wailers. But everyone is loving it, on stage and in the audience. People start dancing in the aisles, including my mother, which would normally horrify me, but this time I don't mind. From the corner of my eye, I see our principal, Mr. Minor, doing some kind of shimmy and a couple of other teachers are following suit. Even Mr. Shuntaro stands up and does a scary-looking shake dance, like he's being electrocuted. The place is hopping!

When we get to our last song, I turn to the audience. "For our final number tonight, we'll be playing the latest song from a great L.A. songwriter—Austin Hirsch, my father." I look down at the reserved seat section, and my dad's jaw drops wide open, like he can't believe what I've done. "The lyrics have been printed out so you can follow along"—I point to the seventh-grade groupie who volunteered to hold up the cue cards I made for the whole song—"so we hope you'll really enjoy this original composition." When the applause dies down, I add: "And I would like to dedicate this song to my grandfather, Saul Hirsch, who is sitting right here in the first row, next to my dad."

Well, this brings the house down more than anything, and

everyone shouts for the two of them to stand up. My dad looks panic-stricken, but Saul gets up like he's been waiting for this moment his whole life, waving to the crowd like the queen of England. At last Dad half stands—all hunched-looking and embarrassed—and the crowd starts laughing. It *is* pretty hilarious.

Grinning from ear to ear, I turn back to the orchestra. "This is our grand finale," I stage-whisper to them. "Let's show 'em what we've got." Like my dad says, punk may be only three chords, but the energy—the energy you can't fake. From the opening chords, we're playing with every cell in our bodies:

I WANNA BE YOUR PARADOX
I WANNA BE YOUR BOBBY SOX,
I WANNA BE YOUR EQUINOX
I WANNA BE YOUR FORT KNOX

YEAH, YEAH, BABY, I WANNA BE YOUR SHOEBOX
LET ME BE YOUR SWEET SHOEBOX

By the second chorus the audience is shouting out the refrain and the orchestra is rocking out: the percussion section is going nuts, horns are pointed up toward the ceiling, the woodwinds are swinging, even the string players are mildly gyrating. Quincy looks happiest of all, playing his double bass

CRISTINA GARCÍA

like it's the last day on earth and keeping his eye on me all the while. I'm sweating like crazy from the heat and the lights and the excitement.

YEAH, YEAH, BABY, I WANNA BE YOUR SHOEBOX
LET ME BE YOUR SWEET SHOEBOX

The audience—led by Mr. Shuntaro—is clapping and stamping to the music so hard, I think it's only a matter of time before a mosh pit breaks out in front. This is it, the real deal, and we're at the center of it. Does it get any better than this?

By the time we finish the song, everyone is on their feet screaming for more. I turn around and look for my dad, and he's sitting there beaming up at me like a lit-up Christmas tree. Saul is next to him, looking the same, and so on down the line to Hiroko, Jim, and my mom, who's still jumping up and down even though the music's stopped. They couldn't look more pleased.

Afterward I'm swarmed with people congratulating me on doing the impossible. I want to share the limelight with Quincy, but I can't find him anywhere—not even by the butter cookies, which sell out in ten minutes. Squid-boy simply disappeared without saying good-bye. I can't figure out why.

Dad sneaks up behind me and gives me the biggest, longest hug I've ever gotten from him. He doesn't say anything, just keeps hugging me like I'll evaporate if he stops. Mom comes over and makes a huge fuss over me too. "That was fantastic, cookie-pie! We're so proud of you!" Jim offers his hand for a shake, but I grab him and give him a hug. He sounds like he really means it when he says, "Congratulations!"

Saul looks tired when I finally catch up with him and Hiroko in the lobby of the auditorium. He's leaning on his cane (Hiroko insisted he use it) and nearly topples over trying to embrace me. "Careful, Daddy, you don't want to fall!" Hiroko warns him, but then she turns and smiles at me. "Good job, Yumi!" Saul's rheumy blue eyes are brimming with pride. "That was some surprise you had in store for us," he jokes. "Darn good song that shoebox, blue box. Heh-heh. I knew you could do it, Yumi girl!" A lot of people have been saying stuff like that to me, but hearing it from Saul is best of all.

I ain't got too much time left, you know. That's why I wanted to see them ships at San Pedro today. There won't be much action on a Saturday, but I still wanted you to come with me. Big ships are a call to adventure, you know what I'm saying? I used to love watching them down by the Brooklyn docks at your age. To see them floating up and down the New York harbor was a thing of beauty. It would get me wondering where they were coming from and who was on board, and the stories would multiply in my head.

What's that I been humming? It's been stuck in my head for

CRISTINA GARCÍA

days now—"Lover Man" by Charlie "Bird" Parker. People say he recorded that song in California, then went off the deep end and started barking like a dog. The blues will do that to you, kid. Nah, I can't do it justice. But it's one of those songs that keeps breaking your heart. Great songs get you looking back at the past. We need them to remember things, good and bad. Sometimes it ain't got nothing to do with the truth. I know that's confusing, Yumi, but trust me, your life is good so far—knock on wood.

So have you thought about law school? What do you mean "no way"? You ever seen a hungry lawyer? You wanna be a musician like your dad? You hear that, Hiroko? We got another starving artist on our hands! But I gotta tell you again, that concert was really something. How much dough did you raise? Five thousand thirty-three dollars? Whoa! Still makes me want to do a jig, and you know I'm not one for dancing. Your mother sure cut the rug pretty good, though!

Don't know how she and Austin got together exactly. He never said nothing. All we know is that one day he calls up and tells us there's someone he wants us to meet. Pretty little thing, your mother, sharp as a tack. The way I heard it was that she interviewed Austin for an article she was doing on the L.A. punk scene. Go figure. Next thing you know, they're getting married. A year later you come along.

Now that was a happy day! Like I been telling you, Yumi, I waited a long time for you. A long time. Prettiest baby ever born. Your mother thought you looked like Hiroko. I didn't see the *resemblance at first, but now I do. You nursed up a storm until you were so big and beautiful that everyone had to stop you in the street.*

It didn't take long for your parents to split up. Me and Hiroko were shocked. You gotta understand that we didn't get no divorces in our day. It happened now and then, but it wasn't normal. But at least one good thing came out of it: Austin started bringing you around every weekend. It was part of the custody arrangement. Hiroko prepared your favorite foods and cleaned the house extra good, in case you put anything in your mouth. We couldn't wait to see you. It's still true. You were born when I was seventy-nine years old, and the last thirteen years have been among the happiest in my life—right up there with my times in Japan and the years my mother was alive.

I was hoping to last a little longer—at least until you graduated high school—but that would put me at ninety-six. Now that's a stretch for anybody. You know what I had for breakfast? Bacon and chocolate ice cream. It ain't like I gotta worry about my cholesterol anymore. Might as well go out with the arteries loaded. Hiroko says I'm eating like a pregnant lady, but it's good to have my appetite back. I try to bargain with her. I say: "Okay, I'll eat some tofu"—you know I can't stand the stuff—"but you gotta take me back to Japan one last time." "Soon, Daddy, soon," she tells me. But soon never comes. If I had the money, I'd get on my own plane.

I know you'd take me if you could, Yumi girl. Thanks a lot for

CRISTINA GARCÍA

that. But I'm only asking you for one thing: Just be here when it's my time, okay? Let me hold your hand. You promise me? You know there ain't nothing more important than your word, little one. You've heard me say it before. You give your word and seal it with a handshake and that should be worth pure gold. I don't mean just for me, but for your whole life. If people don't trust you, you got nothing. You know what I'm saying? Now let's go out and look at them big ships.

MOM PULLS UP TO THE FRONT OF SCHOOL WITH THE convertible top down and my surfboard sticking out of the backseat.

"Surprise!" She waves at me. "I thought you could use a break."

I grin back at her. Sometimes she gets things just right.

At the beach a breeze lifts the waves into a two-foot surf. Midweek there isn't too much action. The pier is quiet and the Ferris wheel is perfectly still. If it were up to me, the beach would be like this all the time. I can concentrate more on my own surfing without worrying what other people think. My wet suit feels tight and itchy, and I turn around and wave at my mom before heading into the surf. "Watch out for sharks!" she shouts. Above us, the sky is blue, but I can see how it browns the farther east it goes. Mom says that every time she looks down on L.A. from an airplane, it looks like a dirty ashtray. Yeah, but it's *our* dirty ashtray.

I'm in the water maybe half an hour, catching a few waves, when I see another surfer paddling toward me. My eyes are cloudy with salt water, but it doesn't take me long to figure out who it is. I want to paddle out to the next break, where I know he can't reach me, but instead, I sit on my board and wait for him. My face must be one tight, scary-looking mask. A part of me wants to shout: *What are you doing here?* I'm not sure where this anger is coming from. Earlier today I missed him something awful.

"Wassup?" Quincy says in that awful rapper accent he refuses to give up.

"Nothin' much. You?" I play along. A chill works its way up my spine, and I clench my jaw so my teeth won't chatter.

"Mind if I join you?"

"It's a free country, dude." I'm furious but try not to show it. All this time I thought *he* was the one who was mad at *me*. I didn't realize it went both ways.

"I guess I owe you an apology," he says, lowering his head.

This breaks down my chill, plus now I'm curious.

"About what?" I ask gently.

"I made a lot of assumptions about you. About us, I mean. And I let my imagination get away with me. I mean, I knew you liked Eli, but I didn't want to admit—"

"I don't like him anymore," I interrupt.

"Yeah, those two are a couple of blowfish. Grosses me out just to look at 'em."

I laugh a little, in spite of myself. Kara finally got Eli to go out with her, and now all they do is kiss behind the jacaranda trees at lunchtime.

"I mean, the saliva just oozes out of their mouths into those long, gooey tentacles." Quincy is on a roll now. "It's like they're building a spiderweb or something."

"Eeeeoooo!" I shriek, and start laughing, harder this time, and he's laughing too. The waves are lapping up against us, and a big one turns him and his board over.

"Sooo," he comes up, shaking water. "Who do you like now?"

His eyes are so green in this light—and hopeful-looking. I wish I could say to him, *You, it's you I like,* and kiss him like it's some big romantic moment in a movie. But I don't feel it, and I don't want to lie to him. To lie to someone is to disrespect them, Saul says. I wait a long time, and I look at him like I would a really good friend, and I smile.

"Me," I answer. "I really like me."

Later Mom drives me over to my dad's place. I'm getting ready to go with him on a piano tuning gig when Hiroko calls and says Saul isn't doing too well, that we should head up straightaway. Hiroko is hardly an alarmist, so Dad is stressed out all the way up to their house. He almost forgets to tell me the good news: that "I Wanna Be Your Shoebox" is getting some airplay on 103.1. Apparently, some sixth grader's father loved the song at our concert. He's a music producer and a friend of Steve Jones and got him a copy of the song. Well, Jonesy must've really liked it because he played it twice today, rhyming the lyrics with the name of his show, *Jonesy's Jukebox*. The other deejays are picking up on it, and word is spreading about the song. Normally, my dad would be ecstatic—isn't this what he's been waiting for his whole life?—but he's too worried about Saul to enjoy it.

When we get there, Saul seems disoriented. His voice is weak and his skin looks papery thin. He's mumbling angrily about Pearl Harbor and President Nixon and making no sense at all. Millie is barking at him, trying to get his attention, but he doesn't pay her any mind. All the excitement wears him down, and Saul shuffles off to take a nap. He doesn't seem to realize that it's eight o'clock at night.

"Poor Daddy," Hiroko mutters, shaking her head. "He been like this all day. Wanting this, wanting that, then changing his mind. Walking around in circles, nervous-nervous. I tell him he too old to get excited. He want heart attack on top everything? 'Be patient, Daddy,' I tell him, but he don't listen. Stubborn old man." She looks sad as she says this. "When he wake up, he forget everything. I give him some barley soup. He feel better. You hungry, Yumi?"

I nod, and that sets Hiroko in motion. She's happiest when she's busy. She prepares avocado sushi for me and fries up some sweet

CRISTINA GARCÍA

potato tempura. Lots of rice with sesame seeds on the side.

"Yumi!" Saul shouts for me twenty minutes later. He's still agitated and talking about Pearl Harbor.

"Guess what?" I interrupt him gently. "My dad's song was on the radio today."

"What song is that, Yumi girl?" This seems to snap him back to the present.

"It's called 'I Wanna Be Your Shoebox.' Remember, we played it at our concert? It's really funny and Steve Jones played it on his show today."

"Oh yeah?"

"Isn't that amazing?"

"No kidding. How does it go again?" Saul is curious now, looking at me intently.

"You know I can't sing."

"Just a few bars, kid."

"Okay, here goes, but it sounds a lot better with the music." I start off in a low voice:

I WANNA BE YOUR PARADOX
I WANNA BE YOUR BOBBY SOX,
I WANNA BE YOUR EQUINOX
I WANNA BE YOUR FORT KNOX.

YEAH, YEAH, BABY, LET ME BE YOUR SHOEBOX
LET ME BE YOUR SWEET SHOEBOX

"Kind of bluesy, eh?" Saul tries to whistle along.

"You need to give it more of an edge," I say, grinning.

"Not bad at all. On the radio, you say? Tell your dad to come in here a minute, will you?"

"Daaaaad!" I shout, and Saul laughs.

"I could've done that myself, kid."

My dad comes in tentatively, but Saul catches him off guard.

"Yumi here sang me your new song." He says it like he's never heard it before.

Dad looks embarrassed but doesn't remind him about the concert.

"It's very catchy." Saul's eyes are rheumy-looking, like two milky blue marbles, but the excitement shines through. "I just wanted to say, well, I'm real proud of you. I should've been saying this to you all along—"

"Aw, c'mon, Dad, it's no big deal."

"—because it's true."

They stand there staring at each other for a long time, like they're trying to say everything they've ever felt with one look.

"Okay, you two can hug now!" I chirp, and they both crack up. "Go on!"

And they do. They hug each other for the first time since Secretariat won the Belmont Stakes over thirty years ago. A good, long hug.

Hiroko comes in at that very moment to see what all the

CRISTINA GARCÍA

fuss is about. When she sees Saul and my dad, she gives me a small smile and nods, like she's proud of me, too.

Dad follows Hiroko out the door. His face is kind of a splotchy red, but he looks pleased and sad all at once. Then it's just me and Saul again.

"Good boy, that Austin," Saul says, sniffing and rearranging the pillows on his bed. He throws a couple of the beige ones to the floor, grumbling that it's too crowded for him to sleep. Then he rambles on about horse racing, and the declining quality of newspapers, and how people give up their dreams too easily, and how, in the end, it's just you and the last beat of your heart. "Will you read to me, Yumi girl? That'll help me sleep. We can talk more in the morning. I'll feel better after a good night's sleep. I still got lots of things to tell you."

"What do you want me to read?"

"You pick something out for me."

"My mom gave me some new poetry."

"Never understood poetry." Saul's eyes are getting droopy, and he yawns as wide as a hippopotamus. He doesn't have many teeth left. It's all pinkish gray in there and dry-looking.

"Neither do I. But my mom says you don't have to understand every word. That it's the music that counts, the things it makes you think of . . . things you might not have thought of before."

"Okay, okay, let's hear it." Saul settles in comfortably, his head resting on two pillows, his arms neatly folded over his stomach. He's wearing his winter pajamas, the striped ones with the navy blue piping.

> The wisteria has come and gone, the plum trees
> have burned like candles in the cup of earth,
> the almond has shed its pure blossoms
> in a soft ring around the trunk. Iris,
> rose, tulip, hillsides of poppy and lupine,
> gorse, wild mustard, California is blazing
> in the foolish winds of April. . . .

∞∞∞

Sometimes it tears me up to look out the window, Yumi girl. Even out here in the great American suburbs. It's the little things that get to me. Those wildflowers there coming up in your grandmother's rock garden, beating the odds to warm themselves in the sun. Or the birds fighting to get past the netting on her pear trees. Or the sky looking so big and bruised, you think it'll never heal. Sometimes I gotta turn away from so much life because I'll miss it too much.

Now you know I'm a Brooklyn boy—I ain't no granola-eating California hippie, that's for sure—and in Brooklyn you grow up with an appreciation for the underdog. For the little guy who didn't have a prayer but duked it out anyway. It's a hard thing to explain, but I got a soft spot for the scrappy fighters like Kid Chocolate. Ah, kid, I should've taken you to a boxing match before I got too old. Is any of this making sense to you? I don't wanna be talking through my hat.

CRISTINA GARCÍA

Look at Millie. Every time Austin leaves her here, she follows me around. I go to the john, Millie stands right outside the door until I come out. I take a nap, and she waits for me by the bed. She even puts her two paws on my chest to wake me up. Scares me half to death. Millie thinks she's my new nurse—heh-heh. And she's shedding up a storm too, losing her winter coat. Hiroko is on Millie's heels with the vacuum cleaner.

Go turn on the radio, Yumi. Just leave it on the same station. You know what I listen to first thing in the morning? No, not the oldies, though a little Benny Goodman wouldn't hurt. Last chance, kid. You give up? The evangelists! Can't you hear them? Praise the Lord this and hallelujah that! They get my heart pumping. Yeah, those sons of guns are good for my circulation. They get Millie all worked up too, and she barks at the radio.

You wanna know what I worship? The ordinary. The commonplace. A good cup of coffee and a hunk of crumb cake. The way the sun and the moon share the sky sometimes at the end of a day. A nice turn of phrase—not that you see much good writing in newspapers anymore. Even the way Hiroko cleans a toilet is a thing of beauty. Heh-heh. And the look on your face when you tell me a joke? Now that's poetry! Remember those knock-knock jokes you used to tell me when you were a bitty thing? I don't want to get all sentimental on you, but if you forget the little things, there's no real point to the big ones. Besides, the big ones don't come around so much. But the little things? They come around every day.

I guess what I'm saying is this: The world's a big show, and I want to stick around and watch. But you'll see, after I'm gone, it'll go on like nothing's happened. Sun up, sun down. People die every day. It ain't no big deal. That's what I tell myself when I start worrying about it. No point in being afraid. The past may be mine, but the future, Yumi girl, the future is all yours. And change will always be part of it, remember that. You can embrace it, make the most of it, join the dance—or you can sit it out and miss the party. It's your choice.

Look at the color of your hair—like honey, it is. And your eyes could win a beauty contest. Oh, you're gonna be a heartbreaker, all right. I wish I could be around to see the boys suffer. Yes sir, that's what I really want to stick around for. I don't have no final answers, little one. But if you gotta ask yourself a question, you could do worse than this: What do I want to bring to the party? It goes by fast, kid, faster than I thought. Every day turns like a page in a book. The way I see it now is simple: I came to walk the earth and dance a few dances. Maybe it don't get no better than that.

I don't know why my voice is getting so loud all of a sudden. Strange, ain't it? Like all my strength is going up my throat. Ah, I better be quiet a minute. I'm just a little worn down. No, don't call Hiroko. You know how she gets. She'll be wanting to rush me to the hospital, and that's the last place I want to go. I'm through with all that. I'm not some pincushion to be sticking needles in anymore. My legs feel heavy, Yumi. Heavy and empty at the same time. My

CRISTINA GARCÍA

arms, too. Like they can float away. Like one of them big ships at San Pedro.

No, no water. Thanks, I'll be fine. Just give me a minute and we'll look at some of my pictures. Show you why the girls went wild for me. You think it was my curly locks? I told you about bald men, didn't I? Yeah, we should be ruling the world.

Listen to my breath, Yumi. It don't sound too good. I can hear it coming from deep inside my guts. My own breath's cleaning me out like an old rag. Can you hear it? Are you there, Yumi girl? Are you there? Bring your face close to mine. Let me feel your breath. Good, good. Now help me get up. Take my hand, kid. Hold it tight. That's a good girl. Yeah, that's a good girl. . . .

JUNE EPILOGUE

VÉRONIQUE FREAKED OUT WHEN I TOLD HER THAT SAUL DIED right in front of me. *Weren't you scared?* But I told her that my grandfather gave me the best gift before he died: his story. And his story taught me a lot. Not that I'd want to live my grandfather's life—it's his after all. But he took his punches and tried to make the best of things. In his own way, he joined the dance.

I'm so glad I was able to be there and hold his hand. It was something I'd promised him, and my word means a lot. I'm really, really sad that he's gone, but I'm also curious where Saul might end up. I keep thinking about what my mom said about energy getting recycled in the universe for eternity. Saul was restless and wanting to travel, so I'm hoping he might become some kind of migratory bird. That might even be better than a racehorse, I think. There are these terns that go from Alaska to Japan every year. If there's any poetry in death, that's what he'll be. An arctic tern. I can hear his *heh-heh* just thinking about it.

Dad and Hiroko came into the bedroom right after Saul died. Millie climbed on the bed, licked his face, then went to lie down by the fireplace. It wasn't this big drama, the way it would've been on the Cuban side of my family. Hiroko was lovingly matter-of-fact. She said it was a shame that Saul had died just then because she'd planned to cook him a nice steak dinner—steak and a baked potato with fresh rye bread on the side.

I was surprised that Saul's body stayed warm for so long—Hiroko kept sticking her hand down his pajama top to check his temperature—and he had a mildly amused look on his face. We stayed beside him all day, talking to him and remembering funny stories. I'd never seen Dad this animated around Saul. At one point he got teary-eyed remembering them watching Secretariat win the Belmont Stakes back in 1973. I even played a little clarinet for Saul as a good-bye, one of his favorite Benny Goodman tunes, "Sing, Sing, Sing." Hiroko finally closed his eyelids after lunch. Dad arranged for Saul to be picked up by the funeral people at his usual bedtime, ten o'clock. Hiroko gave me his gold watch too, like he'd asked her.

My mother came over in the evening with an apple crisp

she'd baked herself. Hiroko encouraged her to touch Saul's skin, but Mom politely declined. She tried to stay calm, but I could tell she was anxious. "Cubans," she whispered to me later, "don't keep their dead lying around the house." Mostly, Mom hung out in the kitchen eating the apple crisp and drinking coffee, something she never does. This only made her more jittery. At one point I went in to the kitchen and told her everything was going to be okay. Then I held her hand and said something to her I almost never say: "I love you, Mom."

Hiroko and my dad had Saul cremated, just like he wanted. They bought this beautiful Brazilian wooden urn in Japantown, and that's where he's stashed today. He would've liked it, I think. Hiroko's erected a shrine to him in their bedroom—*very* Japanese—and puts a few of the things there that Saul loved best: the daily racing sheet, his reading glasses, and a good cigar. Every day she cooks small portions of his favorite foods and offers them to him, like a god. When Hiroko goes to the market or to run errands, she calls out: *I be back in an hour, Daddy!* It's not crazy or anything. It just helps her get through the day. I guess she really loved him a lot.

It's strange to go up to Saul and Hiroko's house on the weekends now (it'll always be Saul and Hiroko's house to me). Every time I walk through the door, I half expect to see Saul sitting in his usual spot on the sofa and welcoming me with that big, booming voice of his: *Hey, Yumi girl! It's good to see you, kid!* This past Saturday, I added something of my own to Saul's altar—a note with this epitaph:

SAUL HIRSCH WAS HERE
1913–2006
AND HE DANCED

After Saul died, all my own troubles didn't feel like troubles anymore. I've been surfing with Quincy almost every day, and we're great friends again. It's like that weirdness between us evaporated. My surfing is getting respectable enough so that the other surfers on Bay Street have decided that it's okay to talk to me.

You know what I really want to do? Make a movie: a documentary about the longtime surfers in Venice. I want to interview the people who were around during the Dogtown era, who watched the greatest surfers and skateboarders of the time, who shared the waves and the sidewalks with them but didn't become famous themselves. The folks who did it simply for the love of it—and still do. I guess you could call them the unsung heroes of Bay Street.

I love the idea that my film might end up on the same shelf with my favorite surf movies at Vidiots. That some kid twenty years from now might watch it and be inspired. That would be the greatest thing in the world. But could I just go up to these surfers and start asking them questions? What if they didn't want to be filmed? What if they thought I was some no-talent twerp getting in their business?

You know what? I went ahead anyway.

I started doing interviews with the older surfers on the beach, filming them with my mom's movie camera. They're about the coolest people in the world. I love that they're so willing to tell me everything about their lives. But maybe I've just learned to listen better. Because of Saul, I mean.

At school the usual dramas are in full swing, but I'm less interested in them. Kara and Eli broke up during a big fight at lunchtime. Later he came to me with a big bag of Gummi worms—he actually brought me orange ones this time—and asked me if I'd go to the graduation dance with him in a couple of weeks. I thought about it for a moment, then told him, nicely, that I was going "stag."

Véronique's parents are trying very hard to be a good family: They're having dinner together every night, playing Monopoly, renting PG movies that bore Véronique to tears, but at least they don't upset her brother. I tell her that even if her parents do split up in the end, she'll survive it. Change is hard, I say, but it makes you grow, too. That's what Saul taught me. Véronique's foil ball has grown another half foot. Two weeks ago she wrote a letter to the Museum of Modern Art in New York, offering to donate her foil ball to their conceptual arts collection. She hasn't heard back from them yet.

My dad is doing a lot better these days too. "I Wanna Be Your Shoebox" has been getting a lot of airplay in Los Angeles and Cincinnati, of all places, and he was listed in *Bass Player* magazine as one of L.A.'s "Twenty Best Rock and Rollers Over Forty." Dad put a little transistor radio on Saul's altar and leaves it tuned to 103.1 so his father can hear "I Wanna Be Your Shoebox" whenever it comes on the air. Sometimes Dad and I sit there listening to the radio, staring out the window at Hiroko's garden. Fresh blossoms cling to the pear trees, and the birds are usually chirping up a storm, like they want to sing along.

Mom is getting married in Napa on June 24, and then we're moving up there. (She said, though, that I can come down to L.A. every month to see my dad and Hiroko and to continue making my film.) Mom's been bustling around getting ready, and I have to admit she seems pretty happy, a deep-down happy. I promised her that I'd play my clarinet at her wedding, the Mozart piece I love so much. This will be my gift to her. A ton of people are coming out to Napa for the festivities: my other grandparents, Tía Paloma and baby Isabel, and a horde of my Cuban cousins from New York and Miami. Tía Paloma and Isabel are going to stay with us for part of the summer too. All of Jim's family is flying in from the Midwest. His kids are grown, and he already has three grandchildren. Mom says that makes me their aunt, if I want to be. That's another thing I've learned. You can never have too much family.

After the wedding there's going to be a big party with a live band and everything. And you know what? I've already decided something: I'm definitely going to dance.

CRISTINA GARCÍA

ACKNOWLEDGMENTS

SPECIAL THANKS TO JUSTIN CHANDA, EDITOR EXTRAORDINAIRE, for helping bring this story to life. A huge *gracias,* too, to the terrific eighth graders of Grant Sawyer Middle School in Las Vegas (class of 2007) and to their dedicated teachers and librarian: Janet Weinberg, Stacey Wolff, Amanda Debrie, and Sharon Lowell. Finally, to all the wonderful students and teachers of Paul Revere Middle School in Los Angeles, where my daughter happily flourished for three years (2003–2006).

The title of this book was inspired by Catherine Bowman's wonderful, witty poem "I Want to Be Your Shoebox," which I came across in *The Best American Poetry 2005*. I laughed out loud when I read it and the minute I put it down, I also knew it would make a great, tongue-in-cheek punk song. Thank you, Ms. Bowman!